SUDDENLY SINGLE

SUDDENLY SINGLE

SOUTHERN DISCOMFORT
BOOK 3

IAN O. LEWIS

EDITED BY
ANN ATTWOOD

Cruz
PUBLISHING

PROLOGUE
CARTER THREE YEARS AGO

"I'm not getting on that thing." I exclaimed. "You know I'm afraid of heights!"

"Then, why on earth did you want to go skiing? You know, on big, tall mountains thousands of feet above us?" Asher pointed at the white peaks surrounding the valley. "The only way up is in these gondolas."

"Karina told me how much fun Telluride is. But she didn't mention mountains." I huffed. "This haircut she gave me makes my chin look small."

"For God's sake, Carter. You're the best-looking man in Richmond, and that includes your dimpled chin." Asher took my hand and pulled me toward the shiny red gondola. "According to the sign, we'll only be in the air for a few minutes, then we'll…"

"I will hurl if I get in that thing." I crossed my arms over my chest and felt stupid. Ever since I started dating Asher, I'd tried to do all the rich-people stuff he was used to. Taking tennis lessons, joining the very expensive Country Club of Virginia, and now skiing in Colorado. According to my hairdresser,

Telluride was the place to be if I wanted to up my social status. But did I have to be carried hundreds of feet in the air to do it? "I'm dizzy just thinking about it. What if the cable snaps?"

"It won't." Asher sighed, then he held his hand out for me to take. "Let's have a drink first. Maybe that will calm you down."

"You want me to go skiing for the first time, drunk?" I took his hand, and he pulled me away from the gondola and back toward the main street. It reminded me of pictures I'd seen of snowy Switzerland.

"We don't have to go skiing, Carter." Asher murmured. "The whole point of this trip was to get away from our mothers and their friends. We never get to be alone."

Asher had a point. Mom and I worked together as interior designers, while Asher worked at his mother's law firm. Our lives were a constant swirl of bridge games, parties, and family gatherings. And you only learned how to play bridge for love. "So, you won't be mad if I won't go up on that gondola?"

"No." Asher stopped walking, and I bumped into him, nearly knocking both of us down to the icy sidewalk. "I just want to be with you. But who knows, maybe a cocktail will calm you down enough to get on the stupid thing."

———

"I love you, Carter. Please, believe me, I really, really, do."

"Even if I'm not from a wealthy family?" That slipped out of my mouth before I thought about it. It was difficult being his boyfriend sometimes, because his background was so different from mine. I felt like I lacked something that was innate to him, and constantly struggled to act like living in mansions while being waited on by servants was normal.

"I wish you'd stop being weird about that." Asher reached

across the table and took my hand. "I can't help it if I was born a Yates, and you can't help that you were born into, well, a normal family. Though your mother is hardly normal."

I smirked and took a sip of my gin and tonic. "Mom is a unique woman, but my business wouldn't be flourishing without her help. She keeps everything running smoothly, so I can take impromptu trips to Colorado with you."

Asher bit his lip, then squeezed my hand. "You've had three cocktails. Think you can brave the gondola ride now?"

"You really want me to ski for the first time with a buzz?" I giggled, and Asher shook his head and smiled.

"I have a surprise for you on top of Palmyra Peak, and it has nothing to do with skiing." Asher gazed into my eyes, unblinking, and my pulse ticked up. Whenever he surprised me with something, it was always out of this world. Just a month ago, he'd blindfolded me, dragged me to the airport, and two hours later we were sitting in the Metropolitan Opera House in New York City. I hated opera, but damn, talk about an over-the-top treat.

"Fine." I emptied my glass and Asher signaled the waiter for the check. "But if I get sick hundreds of feet in the air, you're paying for the victim on the ground's cleaning bill."

———

We had the gondola to ourselves, thank God, and I kept my eyes shut the entire ride. "I'm going to throw up, I can feel it."

"You're fine, baby, only two more minutes." Asher kissed my cheek. "I can see the station where we are landing."

"It feels like we're on a wobbly boat." I opened my eyes for a second and saw Asher typing something on his phone. His lips twisted for a moment, then he shoved the phone back into the pocket of his beige parka. The gondola shook, and my eyes snapped shut again. "We're going to die!"

"No, baby. Trust me, we're going to be just fine." I felt his breath hot against my cheek. A moment later, the gondola shook like we were in the middle of an earthquake. "We're docking at the station, that's all. Open your eyes, and you'll see everything's okay."

I did as instructed, and was relieved to see he was right. It was strangely empty, except for a single person staring at our gondola. Once we were out of it, the stranger strolled up to us.

"Are you Asher Yates?" It was a woman's voice. She was bundled up in a parka similar to the ones we were wearing. Asher smiled and nodded. "Come with me. We'll be there in less than five minutes."

"Who is she, and where is she taking us?"

Asher didn't respond to my question. Instead, he placed his hand on the small of my back and pushed me forward. Once we were outside the station, I saw what appeared to be two sparkling blue snowmobiles. At least, I thought they were. I'd never seen one outside of the movies before.

"Here are our rides." The woman gestured toward it. "Get in the one on the left and follow me."

"Do you know how to drive one of these things?" I whispered, and sank down into the rear seat of the contraption. It had a seatbelt, so I snapped it in place and clutched the sides.

"Yes. I grew up driving these things around Telluride." Asher grinned and started the engine. Being around him was surreal at times. Like, when we arrived, I expected us to stay at a hotel. A fancy hotel, of course. Instead, we were staying at the family compound, an enormous log mansion with fireplaces you could literally stand inside of. Moments later, we were heading up a mountain.

The sound of swooshing snow and the engines made

conversation impossible, so I tightened my hat and kept my face down to keep it from getting wet. Suddenly, we came to a stop.

"We're here." Asher said. "C'mon, get out and look at the view."

I did as he asked, though when I stood up, I almost fell flat on my ass. My legs were shaking, and I smiled nervously toward Asher and the strange woman. She strolled through the snow until she was a few yards away. Asher gently pushed me forward until we were next to a giant boulder.

"Isn't it amazing." Asher put his arm around me, and for a moment, I forgot how to breathe. "I asked you here for a reason." He murmured, and if I wasn't mistaken, his voice was trembling.

"What is it?"

"Now that we're away from our crazy families, I want to ask you a very serious question." Asher dropped to his knees in the snow. My heart hammered in my chest. He grabbed my gloved hand and stared up at me. "If we were back in Richmond, everyone would make a big fuss over this, and I just want it to be you and me."

"Yes." I whispered. "Go on, ask me."

"Carter Camden, I love you with all my heart and soul. Will you do me the honor of becoming my husband?" Asher asked, and at the same time, a bunch of snow blew on us. He waved his free hand in front of his face while I stared into his cobalt eyes. I opened my mouth to respond, but nothing came out. I wanted to say yes, scream it actually, but it was like I had a sudden onset of laryngitis. "Please, answer me, Carter."

I nodded and croaked out, "Yes, of course, I'll marry you."

Asher leapt to his feet, let go of my hand, and cupped his hands around his mouth. "He said yes!" Asher screamed into the valley lying at our feet. I heard a clapping sound, and remembered the strange woman who'd come with us. She was strolling through the snow toward us when Asher pulled me into his chest and kissed me.

"Gentlemen, are you prepared to do it now? Or do you need…."

"Now." Asher exclaimed, and the biggest smile I'd ever smiled stretched across my cheeks. "You have the license and stuff?" He asked her, and she nodded.

"You planned this all along?" I asked, amazed at the romantic gesture. Asher nodded.

"My name is Linda Crawford and I'm a non-denominational officiant, licensed by the state of Colorado to perform weddings." I heard her say, but I couldn't take my eyes off of Asher. The man I loved more than anything or anyone else in the world was marrying me, a man who'd grown up poor on Richmond's Southside. He could have had anyone he wanted, but he'd chosen me.

"I love you, Asher, more than you'll ever know."

CHAPTER 1

ASHER

"Getting married on that mountain three years ago was the most romantic moment of my life, Asher." Carter reached across the antique wooden table and laid his hand on mine. "But I want a real wedding. You know, with us wearing elegant suits, and perhaps your cousin Margaret, who's adorable by the way, she could be our flower girl. Let's have it at the country club."

Carter mentioned a proper wedding last night and wasn't letting it go. After regaining entry to our bedroom this morning, I was trying to stay in his good graces. I sipped my coffee while figuring a way to talk my husband out of it. Carter had the exasperating habit of latching on to an idea the way a dog won't let go of a bone. Because of his impetuousness, we'd already been on safari in Africa, taken trips to China and France, plus his wardrobe had outgrown our closet. He'd now taken over one of the guest bedrooms, and Carter filled it with racks upon racks of clothes. Some of them still had price tags hanging from them. Totally frivolous. And the thing that got me the most was I couldn't say anything. He paid for it with his own money thanks to his booming interior-design business. Plus, it put a beautiful smile on his face.

"It would be the event of the season." Carter sighed, then started typing on his phone. "I want everyone we love to see us take our vows. Can't you understand how important that is for me? For us? For our families?"

"But…"

"When I was at Saks Fifth Avenue in New York last week, I saw the chicest Dior suits that would look perfect on both of us. Though you might want to cut back on the carbs, Asher. You've porked out a little bit." Carter slid his phone back in his pocket and stared at me expectantly. "Well?"

I loved this man. I really, really, did. But he was making me absolutely insane. "I just don't feel the need to get married all over again. The reason I wanted us to get married in Colorado was to avoid a big, expensive ceremony. Lord knows if our mothers and their friends get wind of us getting remarried, they'd…"

"Why do you think I want a new ceremony? Because Mom and Marjorie both bitch to me regularly about how they wished they'd been there for our wedding." Carter closed his eyes and shook his head dramatically.

It was true. Marjorie, also known as my mother, complained to me incessantly about not being there. And all Carter's mother ever did was bitch about everything under the sun. I didn't know how the ogre had raised such a light-hearted son like Carter.

"You know, sweetheart, locking me out of our bedroom last night isn't exactly the way to sell me on this wedding." I said, though what I left unsaid was how refreshing it was to sleep alone for a change. He'd asked me point blank about a new ceremony, and when I said nothing, he accused me of not loving him and threw me out. As Mom liked to say, Carter was handsome, talented, loving, and an over-the-top drama queen. She loved him to the moon and back, to my chagrin.

"Why would I want to sleep next to a man who doesn't want to marry me?"

"But we're already married!" I jumped to my feet, fists balled up at my sides. "For God's sake, Carter. I love you, and damn it, will you just come out of this bedroom and have breakfast with me and the rest of the family?"

"Fine."

———

When we returned from our wedding in Colorado three years ago, we'd moved into my deceased great-aunt's home at the rear of mother's property. It was a four-bedroom cottage over-looking the James River. I'd wanted to buy our own house, but Mother and Carter wouldn't hear of it. It did save us money, but at what cost?

After we married, I'd always thought Carter and I would have a little more alone time. Instead, we were constantly surrounded by family. Perhaps if our families were more normal, it wouldn't be so bad. But unfortunately for me, they were as crazy as sprayed cockroaches.

What made matters worse was how well Carter fit in with the lunatics. When we first started dating, I'd worried that Mom and Granny wouldn't like Carter. That turned out not to be a problem at all. In fact, I'd swear they loved my husband more than me. Why? Because he was fucking nuts like they were.

"Asher, go on to the main house without me. My hair is misbehaving." Carter called out from the bathroom. "I'll catch up in a few minutes."

"Yes, dear."

I let myself out the front door, got in my car, and drove to Mother's house. The cottage had legally been signed over to Carter and me once Mother learned of the wedding. Secretly, I think she gave it to us to make sure we were always close by. It was ridiculous, since I worked for her at the law firm. But Carter fell in love with the old Tudor stable my dead aunt had converted into a home.

Florida, my mother's maid, was standing at the back door, shaking her head at me when I got out of the car. She was dressed in jeans and a green blouse instead of her usual black and white uniform.

"What's wrong now?"

"You be nicer to that man of yours, Asher. Your mother is fit to be tied, so you'd better be on your best behavior." She huffed, putting her hands on her bony hips. She'd worked for us her entire life, and I was certain she was old enough to retire.

"Y'all love him more than me, don't you?" I sighed, then brushed past her into the tack room and hung my jacket up. "What kind of morning is it, Florida? Bloody Marys or actual juices?"

"Coffee is all you get." She stalked past me into the kitchen. "Your mama said you have an important hearing at the court-house, and she's going with you."

"What?" Damn it. I was officially a partner at Yates, Minor, and Reynolds, but Mom persisted in treating me like I'd just got out of law school.

"You heard me. Now get in the dining room. Your grand-mother wants a word with you about Carter." Florida said as I strolled out of the kitchen.

My family apparently knew about our quarrel from last

night, and they were determined to break me. Whatever. As usual, I'd give in, so I could avoid the drama.

When I entered the dining room, both Mom and Granny scowled at me.

"Fuck it! I'll marry him again!" I pulled my chair out and plopped my ass down. In front of Mom there was a tall glass filled with what appeared to be a Bloody Mary, and a celery stalk poked out the top. "Why do you get to drink a Bloody and I'm stuck with coffee?"

"It's tomato juice, sweetheart." Mom cooly replied, and I knew she was lying. She possessed a liver made of iron.

"Don't curse in front of me." Granny practically poured the entire sugar bowl into her cup of coffee. She had a mouth like a sailor, and would only protest once about language before filth spewed forth from her painted orange lips.

Florida pushed a cart into the dining room with our breakfasts on it. She placed eggs, bacon, waffles, and freshly cut fruit in the center of the table, then poured me a cup of coffee. I reached for a waffle and she swatted my hand. "Only fruit. Carter said he has to go shopping for you because you're outgrowing your clothes."

"I'll eat whatever I want." I snatched a piece of bacon and bit it in half. "Hmm. You're a pain in the ass, Florida, but you're also the best cook in Virginia." I smiled, hoping she'd smile too. Instead, she shook her head in Mom's direction, and pushed the cart out of the dining room.

"Stop cussing, goddamn it."

"Granny, please." I rolled my eyes, then heard a loud whoop come from the kitchen. A moment later, Carter strolled into the dining room with a smiling Florida following behind him carrying a carafe of orange juice. He'd gelled his dark wavy hair to perfection, and I doubted even a tornado would make it budge.

"Carter!" Mom grinned at him.

"Good morning, Carter." Granny tilted her head, a sparkle in her eye. Now that his fan club had greeted him, I prepared for the entire room to gang up on me. Granny sipped her coffee, then lowered her eyes and shook her head in my direction. "Why won't you let us see the two of you get married? Even the event director at the country club thinks it's a fabulous idea for the two of you to…"

"Stop right now. I will not argue about my marriage with all of you." I inwardly groaned, then continued. "If it will make you happy, Carter, we can be remarried. Just please, mind the…"

"Oh, thank God!" Florida placed a hand on her chest and stared up at the ceiling.

"As I was saying, mind the cost. We really don't need new Dior suits, and God knows what else you have up your sleeve." Even though I said what needed to be said, I was prepared to be ignored.

Silence ruled for a few beats, then Carter pulled out the chair across from mine and sat. Florida poured him a glass of juice, then grabbed his plate and filled it with everything she'd forbidden me from eating.

His lips twisted, then he spoke, "Why are you hesitating? Like, do you even want to be married?" His eyes were wet, and I knew if I didn't calm him down, he'd have a major meltdown within seconds.

"Of course I do." I glanced around the table, and his fan club were all clucking their tongues at me. "Carter, you know I love you." I speared a wedge of cantaloupe off the tray and wished it was sausage.

"I don't believe you." Carter salted his eggs, then poured maple syrup on his waffles. "Tell me the truth. If we had to do it all over again, would you still marry me?"

I blinked, suddenly hyper-aware that if I said the wrong thing, I would be outnumbered by Carter and my insane family.

"Well, come on, answer the question." Carter sighed. "Would you still marry me?"

CHAPTER 2

ASHER

Fuck me.

If I spoke the truth, Carter would be pissed. If I lied, he'd see through it in a split second.

"Go on, answer him." Florida squinted her eyes. I glanced over at Granny, and she had a strange expression on her face, like she wanted me to say the wrong thing. My family lived for drama, and usually I could bluff my way out of stuff. I wasn't so sure this time. Mom cleared her throat and placed her napkin next to her plate.

"No."

Everyone gasped.

"But it isn't for the reasons you think, Carter." I jabbered, my brain spinning to find the right words.

"Really?" Carter pushed his plate to the side and stared daggers at me.

"Yes. You see, I love you very, very much. We don't need a fancy wedding to prove my love for you to the world." I stood and walked around the table until I was right behind him. I began massaging his shoulders, and Carter slapped my left hand.

"That's all fine and good, but what about my needs?" Carter gestured toward Mom and Granny. "And what about the needs of your family? They all want a wedding, to see the most important day of our lives for themselves."

"You asked me a question, and I spoke the truth." I walked to the other side of the room and leaned against the wall so I could see Carter's expression. His normally tan skin was beet red, and he began drumming his fingers on the table. "I'm not lying when I say I love you more than anything else on this planet, Carter. I just don't feel like marriage is necessary, that's all."

"Darling, it would make me and Mother so happy to see the two of you walk down the aisle together." Mom said, then drained her alleged tomato juice. "Your father, God rest his soul, would have wanted to see you married too. Florida, would you mind?" Mom pointed at her empty glass. "Make it with the special sauce in the pantry, dear."

I rolled my eyes as Florida took the glass and raced to the kitchen. The special sauce was code for vodka.

"Why do I get the feeling you regret marrying me in the first place?" Carter steepled his fingers under his chin, his eyes as wide as tennis balls. At least he didn't resemble a ripe tomato now.

"Sweetheart, when I made those vows on Palmyra Peak, I meant every word. I love you more now than I did then, and I want you by my side for all eternity." I met Carter's gaze, which softened for a split second before turning flinty again.

Florida walked in and placed a glass of tomato juice next to Mom's hand. It was suspiciously pink, meaning it had an extra shot or three of vodka. How Mom made it to the office every day was a mystery. Thankfully, she rarely drove herself. She took a sip, and a slow smile spread across her cheeks. "Thank you, Florida. Asher, would you mind giving me a lift to work, dear?"

"Of course I will." I sighed. If I hadn't, Florida would be pressed into driving duty.

"Back to me, please." Carter said, and I felt sweat dripping down my sides. Mom and I had a meeting in less than an hour with Judge Gottwald about a civil suit he was recusing himself from. At this rate, I wouldn't have time to look over my notes. Wait a minute. Didn't Mom and the judge date back in high school?

"Oh, Mom, you want to see the judge because… that's why you're coming with me to the courthouse." It occurred to me that she and the Judge were both widowed, and around the same age. She winked at me, then turned to Carter.

"Darling, Asher has agreed to the wedding. Unfortunately, we have a meeting with Judge Gottwald in a matter of minutes." Mom slugged the rest of her drink back, and I felt in my pockets to make sure I had mints handy. She was going to need them. "Lucky for us, you're the most talented interior designer in Virginia, and I'm sure you know the best wedding planners. Why don't you start working on the service and the reception. Oh, and let Mother help. She loves throwing parties." She nodded at Granny, whose eyes lit up.

I pushed myself off the wall and sat next to Carter. "Honey, I'll do whatever you want. Start planning the service, just, you know, keep the costs reasonable."

Carter's gaze focused somewhere over my shoulder, not meeting my gaze. "Whatever you say, Asher."

———

"That went well, dear." Mom smiled and opened the door to my silver Jaguar. "In fact, Thom said he wanted to discuss the case over dinner." She sat and buckled the seat belt.

"Both of us?" I was confused. Mom had done most of the talking with Judge Gottwald, and I'd already decided to just let her handle the case.

"Of course not, Asher." Mom pulled a tube of hot-pink lipstick out of her purse, then adjusted my rear-view mirror to apply it. "Thom sent me a text message as soon as we left his office. I checked my phone in the ladies' room. We're meeting at Lemaire this Saturday for dinner." She opened her purse and dropped the lipstick inside while I repositioned the mirror. "Your father died five years ago, and I want to relaunch myself socially."

"It's about damn time." I grinned at Mom, and she reached over and ruffled my hair. My mother was certifiable, but she had mourned long enough. "Maybe we can have a double wedding."

"Bless your heart, Asher." Mom chuckled. "No. Never again. I told myself before marrying your father that I'd only get married once. But, I miss the companionship of a man. Marriage is hard work. All I want is a good friend, and perhaps a smidgen of romance."

I pulled out of the parking lot of the courthouse and a moment later we were on Broad Street, heading to our offices downtown. Mom's words danced around my head, and I realized Mom probably knew exactly how I felt about my marriage.

"Mom, I love Carter, but he's so demanding." I sighed, and Mom patted my arm. "I'll do anything to make him happy, including having another ceremony. But can I tell you something in confidence?"

"Of course, Asher."

"If I had to do it all over again, I wouldn't have married him."

Mom cleared her throat. "You mentioned that at breakfast. Whatever do you mean?"

"I can't imagine my life without him, but there's always so much drama." The right words wouldn't come to me, so I just blurted out whatever came to mind. "I knew he would be a handful. In fact, that's one reason I love him so much. Never a dull moment."

"Well, he fits in beautifully with the family." Mom's voice slurred. "While I never expected you to settle down with a man, I can't imagine our family without Carter in it."

"Oh, Mom, neither can I." I flipped the turn signal and made a right onto Belvedere. "I'm just saying that if I had to do it all over again, I'd just want to shack up. You know, live in sin with him, instead of…"

"Darling, that's a marriage. Even though the Commonwealth of Virginia doesn't recognize common-law marriage, we have won huge settlements for clients who cohabitated." Mom pointed out the window as we drove past the Virginia War Memorial. She always did, because that was where Dad proposed to her. "So, getting married is helpful, because legally it gives you a precise idea of…"

Mom droned on and on about the legal benefits of marriage, despite her saying earlier she'd never do it again herself. But I was used to the contradictions. My entire family was riddled with them. When I turned into the parking deck of our building, she finally dropped the subject.

"Asher, Florida is picking me up. She wants me to go along with her on a doctor's appointment." She opened the car door and stepped out. "It's only a check-up, but I always worry about her. She's more than a maid to us. Florida is family."

"Of course."

When we got to our offices on the fifteenth floor, Mother turned left down the hallway, waving to the receptionist. I turned right, and moments later said good morning to my secretary, Gloria.

"Mr. Yates, there's an important letter on your desk. A courier delivered it a few minutes ago." Gloria joined the firm when I did, seven years ago. Unlike the rest of the women in my life, she was decidedly not the motherly type. I adored that about her.

"Thank you, Gloria. Hold my calls for the next fifteen minutes while I prepare for the day." I scooted into my office, then saw the envelope sitting in the center of my desk. In bright red ink, the word URGENT was stamped on it. I laid my briefcase down, then ripped it open.

Dear Mr. Yates,

I am writing to let you know of an unfortunate mistake made by Linda Crawford and the State of Colorado. According to our records, she hadn't renewed her license to officiate weddings by the deadline set by state law. Because of this, your marriage to Carter Camden is not valid. We apologize for....

"Oh my fucking God!"

I grabbed the letter and raced out of the office. "This is a disaster. No calls!" I shouted, running past Gloria's desk. When I got to Mom's office, her secretary tried to stop me, but I pushed open the door.

"Asher, what's wrong?" Mom took her gold reading glasses off, her brow furrowing. We never barged into each other's offices like this.

"I,I,I, um, shit." I gave her the letter, and she put her glasses back on.

"Oh dear." Mom scanned it, then let the paper drop to her desk. She stood up and crossed the room to the mini-bar in the corner.

"Whatever you're having, make me a double." I muttered, and the sound of ice dropping into glasses filled the air. "What the hell am I going to do, Mom? Carter is going to flip out."

"Here. Take this." She handed me the glass of clear liquid. I shot half of it back and wheezed. Vodka on the rocks, no mixer. Mom sat behind her desk and picked up the letter. "This is a technicality, and if worse comes to worst, you could sue the state of Colorado for negligence. But..."

"Mom, if Carter discovers we've never been married, he'll have a complete breakdown. Like, you know how high-strung my husb...I mean Carter is. Shit, we're not married." I put my face in my hands and took deep breaths. Now that we weren't married, I felt empty. Damn it, if I could take back what I said to Carter at breakfast, I would. There was nothing I wouldn't do for him. I glanced back up at her and opened my mouth, but she held a hand up to stop me.

"I'm putting my lawyer hat on now, Asher." Mom drained her drink, setting the empty tumbler down on her desk with a thud. "Don't say a word about this to Carter."

"What?"

"Honey, Carter is family, and we all love him. But this might come in handy one day if you and he hit a rough patch." Mom leaned back in her chair and eyed me.

"But I don't get it." Pressure built behind my eyes. This was a catastrophe.

"If you and Carter ever decide to separate, your assets will be better protected. Of course, we'd never let him leave without a fair settlement, but you must think of the future, son." Mom took her glasses off and shook her head.

"What future? He'll go nuclear if he finds out about this." A sob vibrated through my chest.

Mom steepled her hands under her chin. "Not if we don't tell him, dear."

CHAPTER 3

CARTER

"Damn it." I muttered. Someone was in my clearly marked, personal parking space. Hopefully, they were a paying customer. I pulled into the spot next to it, nearly scraping my hairdresser Karina's yellow Range Rover. She rented the back of the renovated church for her salon, while I used the rest of the building for Camden-Yates Interiors.

When I stepped out of my Mercedes, I noticed three of Karina's hairdressing apprentices hanging out on the back stairs smoking cigarettes. They knew that was a no-no, and I made a mental note to talk to her about it.

"Hi, Mr. Yates!" One of the apprentices called out, and the three of them dropped their cigarettes and raced back inside. I always entered through the rear of the building, and when I was at the top of the stairs, I could still smell tobacco. Definitely had to speak to Karina, because I didn't want my clients to smell smoke on me.

I pushed the back door open, and strolled into the showroom, where Mom was helping a customer pick out throw pillows. While I worked exclusively with interior design, my mother managed the showroom and acted as my assistant. She waved and grinned at me as I breezed past them into the office. After hanging up my coat, I checked my calendar, then heard the click clack of Mom's stiletto heels approaching.

"Darling, I talked that woman I was helping into setting up a consultation with you. She wants to enlarge her dressing room. Should be a piece of cake." Mom grinned, and as always, I couldn't help but wish her surgeon had been more conservative with her most recent nose job. Every time she smiled, I could see up her nostrils.

"Thanks, Mom." I leaned back in my chair and sighed.

"What's wrong?" Mother sat across from me in a Chippendale chair I'd found at an estate sale. "You look like someone kicked your dog."

"Mom, the last twenty-four hours have been hellish, to say the least." I groaned. "Asher doesn't want me anymore."

"Don't be ridiculous." Mom smoothed out her skirt. "It's the stress of living with his snobby family. If the two of you could live away from them, I'm sure things would settle down. Lord, his mother, Marjorie, always looks down her nose at me."

She did, but I couldn't let Mom know that. For whatever reason, my mother-in-law disliked Mom. But she was always polite to her. I suspected Marjorie loved being the headstrong matriarch, while Mom also preferred being in charge. There wasn't room for two queens in our family, and Mom was acutely aware of it.

"I saw Marjorie last week at Karina's getting a blowout. She had the nerve to ask me if I'd had a facelift." Mom stood up and began pacing in front of my desk. "I told her that aside from a little tweak here and there, I'd never had any sort of major surgery."

I rolled my eyes. When Mom crossed her legs her mouth

automatically snapped open. "Mom, at breakfast this morning, I asked Asher if he had to do it all over again, would he still marry me."

"And?" Mom raised a perfectly painted-on eyebrow.

"He said, no, he wouldn't."

"Oh my God." Mom sank into the chair and fanned herself. The skin on her neck was bright red. I stood and got a bottle of cold water out of the mini-fridge behind the little bar in the corner. Mom insisted she wasn't going through the change, but it was plain as the non-surgically altered nose on my face that she was. "Thanks, Carter."

I sat down and cradled my face in my hands for a moment. "Mom, Asher doesn't love me anymore. I can tell."

"Oh baby, he probably woke up on the wrong side of the bed." Mom said, then drained half the bottle of water at once.

"Make that the wrong side of the couch. I kicked him out of the bedroom last night."

"Why?"

"Because, when I asked him if we could get remarried, so our families could actually watch us, he said no. I mean, why would I want to share the bed with someone who doesn't want to be married to me?" I grimaced. "Then at breakfast this morning, and by the way, Marjorie was already tipsy when they left for the office, he said he wished we'd never been married."

"That bitch needs AA." Mom winked, and I wondered if I could see the inside of her brain through her prominent nostrils. Nothing made her happier than hearing the sordid details of Asher's family. "And sweety, you're already married. It's not like he's asked you for a divorce."

"What if I want one?" I huffed. "I take that back. By the end of breakfast, he agreed to have a new ceremony performed. It thrilled his entire family, of course, and his grandmother is helping me plan it."

Mom lowered her eyes and sniffed.

"Oh, and you're helping too. The event planner at the country club thinks a ceremony there would be perfect." I grinned, hoping to smooth things over. Mom thought the Yates hated her and deliberately left her out of certain family activities. They didn't hate her, but they didn't know exactly how to fit her into their family. Mom was a loud dresser and a talker. The Yates were old money, and Mom felt insecure when she was around them.

Mom sighed, then we heard the bell ring, which indicated someone had come inside the showroom. "Let me help the customer, sweetheart."

———

"The materials just arrived, Carter." Beverly Southall barked over the phone. "When does construction start?"

"Give me one moment." I checked my calendar, and saw that our contractors weren't scheduled to start until two weeks from today. Beverly was a pushy older woman who lived a mile down River Road from the Yates estate. She'd want me to bump up her job to tomorrow, if possible. "The crew isn't available for two more weeks. But, if we have any cancellations, I'll…"

"Oh please, if at all possible, move it up. It's so tacky having all this wood and bricks taking up space in the driveway." I heard her inhale and suspected it was a contraband cigarette. Her husband was the president of the local lung association, and I'd seen him snatch a lit cigarette out of her mouth in public on more than one occasion. Thankfully, there was a knock on the door. "Beverly, I've got to go, um, my next appointment is here." I hung up before she could say anything else. The door swung open, and a man strolled in, with Mom following along behind him.

"Are you Carter Camden Yates?"

"Yes." I glanced at Mom, who shrugged her shoulders.

"This is for you." The man laid an envelope in front of me marked URGENT, then spun around and marched past Mom out of my office.

"Wait!" I called after him, but a moment later we heard the bell ring, which meant he'd exited the store. "What is this?"

Mom eyed me. Then the bell rang again, so she raced back into the showroom.

I snatched up the mother-of-pearl letter opener Asher gave me. My gut clenched, then I sliced the envelope open.

Dear Mr. Camden,

I am writing to let you know of an unfortunate mistake made by Linda Crawford and the State of Colorado. According to our records, she hadn't renewed her license to officiate weddings by the deadline set by state law. Because of this, your marriage to Asher Montgomery Yates is not valid.

"What the fuck?" I muttered, the paper falling from my hands. "This can't be happening!" I raced to the showroom, where Mom was ringing up a customer. As soon as the woman left with her lamp, I locked the shop doors.

"Honey, what's wrong?" Mom asked while my stomach churned. "Was it the letter, that man…"

"Yes!" I grabbed her hand and dragged her back to my office. "Read it." I pointed at the paper on my desk, not wanting to touch it again. Mom picked it up, her lips moving as she read.

"This can't be true." Mom's eyes widened. "I can't believe this."

"Asher and I are done for." I felt tears building up and swiped at my eyes. "He's already said he wished he'd never married me. Well, his wish just came true." Damn it, I loved him so much, and now it turned out we'd never been legally married at all.

"Now, now, Carter. Let's not make rash decisions." Mom crossed over to the bar and pulled out two mini-bottles of wine we saved for customers. She didn't even bother with glasses, just twisted open the bottle and chugged. "What if he doesn't know? Like, maybe they only sent the one letter to you." She handed me the other bottle, and I downed the contents at once.

"I don't want to be married to him anymore. He doesn't love me. I know it." I sat behind my desk and a tear slid down my cheek.

"Darling, it's just the shock talking. As soon as you calm down, you'll see that you need to be with Asher, even if he belongs to that snobby family." Mom sat down, then pulled a tissue out of the box on my desk and handed it to me. "You know how I feel about the Yates family, but it would be social suicide to leave Asher."

"God, Mom." I mopped up my face with the tissue. "I'm not staying married, I mean, I'm not staying with Asher just so I can..."

"They'll toss you out of the Country Club of Virginia, and you'll lose many of your wealthy clients." Mom shook her head back and forth. "You've got to admit, this business took off after you became a Yates."

My mother was the real snob, not the Yates family. She was only interested in my last name, not my happiness. But would I ever be happy without Asher by my side? I loved him more than anything else in this world.

"Darling, just don't say a word to Asher or his family. And definitely say nothing to any of your friends or clients. When you two have your new ceremony, you can make sure it's legal and binding. Nobody will be the wiser, and…"

"Mom, how can I not tell Asher about this? He's a lawyer, and he'll…"

"Keep your trap shut, Carter." Mom snapped. "And all of this nonsense will fade away." Mom came around the desk and started rubbing my shoulders. "Do you trust Mommy?"

"Jeez, Mom, I'm thirty-two years old. Stop talking to me like I'm a baby." I sighed. "Fine, I'll say nothing for now. But if he says one more time that he wishes we weren't married, I'm out the door."

CHAPTER 4

ASHER

The smell of autumn was in the air, and despite the chilly temperatures, I kept the car windows down as I drove home from work. The sun was setting earlier, and I wanted nothing more than to slip into my pajamas and call it a night. Maybe Carter and I could start a fire, and share a few quiet hours alone, without family interference. But how on earth was I supposed to keep our non-marriage a secret from him? He owned my heart, and keeping secrets from each other was unheard of.

"Damn it." I shook my head as I drove past Mom's house. Lila Brooke and Mary Jane's silver Bentley was parked next to Florida's minivan. As soon as they knew I was home, they'd summon me to come have a drink or play cards. All I wanted was to be alone with Carter, but if I turned the ladies down, I wouldn't hear the end of it for days.

When I reached our cottage, my phone buzzed. After switching off the car, I picked it up and saw a message from Carter.

Running late

Emergency appointment with Belinda
Therapista

"Shit." Carter must be super-stressed out if he went to see his shrink. The woman's real name was Belinda Johnson, but since she had a definite resemblance to the supermodel Linda Evangelista, Carter insisted on calling her that nickname. I hoped I wasn't the reason for his emergency therapy session, but most likely I was.

"How am I supposed to keep this news about our marriage from him?" I slammed my car door shut and went into the cottage.

A stack of mail was on the kitchen counter, and as usual, it was all bills. I left them for Carter since they were his and dropped my briefcase in the small home office. Carter decorated the cottage, in what he called the first families of Virginia style. Antiques, mingled with contemporary art he'd found at various art galleries up and down the east coast. Since restraint was an unknown word for Carter, our living space was crowded. A few weeks ago he'd mentioned adding a few rooms to the cottage, designed by him, of course. At first I'd put my foot down, saying it was too expensive. But on second thought, a project might be just the answer to my problem. Keeping Carter busy would make it easier to avoid the topic of our non-marriage.

"Asher! Where are you?" Florida's voice came from the kitchen, where she'd let herself in.

"Be right there." I shouted, then ran to the bedroom and took my suit and tie off. Normally, I'd put on a simple pair of jeans and a polo shirt. But I decided to wear this fancy outfit Carter bought for me a few weeks ago. Who knows? It might make him happy. According to the label, somebody named

Marc Jacobs designed it, and to my dismay, it was snug around the waist. Maybe Carter was right, and I'd put on a few pounds?

Florida was washing dishes when I strolled into the kitchen. "You don't have to do that." I took the dish towel from her hands. "Corinne is coming tomorrow. She'll take care of the dishes."

"I don't trust her." Florida shook her head.

"She's your niece." I grinned. "So, what do I owe this honor?"

"The ladies need you up at the big house." Florida grabbed hand cream off the windowsill over the sink and squeezed some into her hands. "Your Momma is running late, and they need a fourth for bridge."

"Okay." I forced a smile. I'd hoped Carter and I could have a few moments of peace together, but that wasn't happening if Lila Brooke and Mary Jane were here. "Oh, how did your doctor's appointment go? Are you alright?"

"Oh yes, Dr. Spencer says I'll live to be a hundred. But they found a suspicious mole on my back and had to do a biopsy," She said. "Now don't worry about me. Let's get to the big house before the ladies are too drunk to play cards."

———

"Where's Mom?" I asked, sitting across from Lila Brooke. She had a pad of paper next to her and wrote my name down. Apparently, we were to be on the same team. A martini was in front of her, and she was wearing her usual uniform. Green and pink kilt, with a white blouse and a pink cardigan hanging over her shoulders. Her white hair was in a loose bun on top of her head, held in place by shiny black chopsticks.

"Marjorie had a last-minute thing come up, something to do

with a board of directors?" Mary Jane, Lila Brooke's longtime companion, shrugged her shoulders. Everyone knew they were lovers, but for the last forty-odd years, they'd kept up the charade that they were nothing more than roommates. Mom once told me it had something to do with Lila Brooke's inheritance. She couldn't come out and keep her money because of a bigoted father. "Want a brownie?" Mary Jane held a plate up, but I shook my head no. She was the only non-alcoholic in the room, preferring pot brownies and other edibles she cooked up regularly. At least she lived up to her name.

"Let's stop the chatter and play bridge." Granny began dealing the cards. Lila Brooke and Mary Jane were her besties, and the three of them had gone to Vassar together. According to Mom, the three of them had been wild at school, notorious even for the swinging sixties. Whenever I asked Granny about her college days, she'd waggle her eyebrows and say nothing.

"Darlings, sorry I'm late." Mom swept into the room and kissed the top of my head. "Have you started yet?" Mom asked, referring to the card game.

"No. Why don't you take my place, Mother." I got up, and Mom slid into my chair. Lila Brooke's smile split her face. She hated losing, and thought Mom was a card shark. What they didn't know was that Mom and Florida had a system for cheating. Mom told me about it once after a few too many cocktails, and swore me to secrecy.

"Here, sugar." Florida handed me a tumbler filled with clear liquid. "Carter said you can only drink vodka or gin. Something to do with carbs or calories." Then she made her way around the table while the ladies examined their cards. No one realized Florida was examining their cards too. Granny made the opening bid, and Florida went to the bar and started making drinks. Though I didn't know the particulars about their cheating system, I knew that if she handed

Mom a whiskey, that meant her opponents held a certain card. If it was a clear liquor, that meant they were holding something else entirely. Ice cubes also had something to do with it.

"I'm going to win this time, I swear it." Mary Jane eyed my mother. They had to know something was sketchy, since they almost never beat Mother's team. I wondered what would happen when they all found out that Mom and Florida were in cahoots.

"Good luck, Mary Jane." Mom drawled. "May the best woman win."

"Ladies." Carter entered the room, and I noticed his shoulders were slumped. When he saw me, he flinched, then strolled over and pecked my cheek.

"Carter!" Florida grinned, then raced to the bar to make him a cocktail. When she returned, she gave him his usual gin and tonic, then she strolled over and placed a whiskey on the rocks next to Mother. The game was officially on.

"How come you're late, Carter dear?" Lila Brooke asked. "Long day at work?"

Carter glanced over at me and sighed dramatically. "No, I had to check in with Belinda Therapista. Stress, you know, the usual." Carter sat on the loveseat opposite the card table, and I sat next to him and patted his knee.

"Is everything okay?" I whispered, and he turned and looked at me like I was a specimen under a microscope. He opened his mouth and nothing came out. "I love you, no matter what it is."

"Do you?" Carter whispered back. When his gaze met mine, I saw his eyes were wet. Whatever he was going through couldn't be worse than how I was feeling. Learning about the legal mixup surrounding our wedding was eating me alive. Mom told me to stick to my guns and not say a word to Carter until she'd examined my options. Since she was the best lawyer in Virginia, I was reluctantly following her advice.

"Of course I do." I sighed, then glanced up and saw Mom staring at us. She returned her gaze to the cards in her hands, and Florida removed her empty tumbler of whiskey and replaced it with what appeared to be a vodka on the rocks. Since it was ill-advised to mix clear liquors with brown, I wondered how none of the other women had figured out Mom and Florida's system.

"You know Marjorie cheats, don't you?" Carter whispered, and when I looked at his face, he almost looked like his old mischievous self.

"Oh yes." I pecked him on the cheek. "Wouldn't expect anything less from good old Mom. So, tomorrow's Saturday. What have you planned for us this weekend?"

"Nothing." Carter tilted his head, a far off look in his eyes. "Mom and I are going to Charlottesville tomorrow for an estate sale. Need to restock inventory for the showroom."

"Did I hear you're going to Charlottesville?" Lila Brooke called out. "Mary Jane and I are too. We're having lunch at the downtown mall with her cousins. Maybe you could join us?"

"I'll have to ask my mother and see if she's up for it." Carter replied, and I noticed Mary Jane and Lila Brooke sharing a knowing glance. They mustn't have heard that his mother was coming too.

"Oh, don't bother her, dear. This is a last-minute thing, you know what I mean." Mary Jane drawled.

———

"Good night, Carter." I switched off the lamp on the nightstand next to me. Normally he'd be cuddling up next to me, but tonight he was keeping to his side of the mattress. Somehow, I needed to reassure him I still loved him. But it was almost impossible to do when he erected these walls between us.

"Actually, I'm going to borrow your office and get a little work done." Carter got out of bed and went to the door. "Busy day at work. Didn't finish everything I needed to."

"Are you...?" The door shut before I could finish my sentence. I punched my pillow, turned over, and sighed.

"He knows. I swear Carter knows. But how?"

CHAPTER 5

ASHER

When I woke up, Carter wasn't in bed with me, and I wondered if he'd slept in one of the other bedrooms. He knew something was up, and despite Mom's opinion that I should keep my mouth shut, I wondered if I should just tell Carter the news. I had no problems marrying him again now that we weren't legally married. Yes, Carter was a handful, but the thought of him being out of my life terrified me.

I swung my feet to the floor, then stood up and stretched. Carter's robe wasn't hanging on the back of the closet door like it usually was, so maybe he was still in the house somewhere.

"Good morning!"

"Jesus!" I jumped at the sound of Carter's voice. "You scared the hell out of me."

I turned back to the door, where Carter stood with his usual perky morning smile. "Coffee first." I muttered. Carter surprised me by flinging his arms around my shoulders, and squeezing me tight. "Where did you sleep?"

"Next to you, silly. I had to get up early because of my day trip to Charlottesville with Mom." He pecked my cheek and let go of me. "And I made us breakfast."

I smiled. Breakfast away from the asylum. "Wow. To what do I owe this distinct pleasure?" Carter grabbed my robe and held it open for me. I stepped into it, and he tied the knot.

"Well, I took a stroll earlier, and noticed Lila Brooke and Mary Jane's Bentley still parked up at the main house. Which means…"

"The party went on until the wee hours." I chuckled. The older ladies party harder than we do. "Nobody is awake to make food, because they kept Florida busy half the night."

"Yep, and I'm starving. So I let myself into your Mother's kitchen and borrowed a few things from the fridge." Carter took my hand and led me toward the stairs. "I hate to eat and run, but I'm picking up Mom in half an hour."

We headed down the stairs, and with every step, I felt guiltier. Carter was still holding my hand, and had gone out of his way to prepare breakfast for us. Though that probably meant half a grapefruit and black coffee for me.

"Sit, sit." Carter pointed at the kitchen table where two plates were sitting. I smelled bacon and prayed it wasn't just for him. A moment later, Carter set a large veggie omelet in front of me, which included two strips of tasty bacon. "Don't you play tennis with your lawyer friend Cort later this morning?"

"Shit. I forgot." I crunched the bacon between my teeth.

"That's why you're getting an enormous meal. You'll need energy to kick his ass." Carter smiled, then reached over and cut a small slice of omelet and set it on his plate. "Plus, I'm sorry if I made you feel bad about gaining weight. It wasn't my intention. I just know your father died of a heart attack, and…"

"Honey, it's okay. Thanks for worrying about me." I said, and my inner guilt ramped up. Damn it, Carter cared for me. How could I keep such a massive secret from him? If he found out I deliberately didn't tell him we weren't married, he'd have a nervous breakdown. Damn it, I needed to 'fess up before it's too late.

I opened my mouth to speak, and nothing came out.

"Yes?" Carter washed down the last of his omelet with a sip of juice. "What were you going to say?"

I shut my eyes, trying to find the right words to break it to him, but a vision of Mother filled my head instead.

"Not if we don't tell him, dear."

"So, what are you and Sissy doing in Charlottesville today?" I couldn't look him in the eye

"Mom and I are going to an estate sale. It's actually in Crozet, outside of C'ville." Carter stood and grabbed his empty plate and rinsed it. "Is Corinne coming today?"

"Who?" My mind blanked, then realized he was talking about the maid. "Yeah, just leave the dishes in the sink. She'll take care of it."

"Awesome." He glanced at his watch, then came over and kissed me on top of my head. "I've gotta hurry. Have fun playing sports ball at the club."

———

When I parked the car, Cort was leaning against his green Porsche, eying his watch. "Did you eat yet? Because I'm starving."

"Yes, Carter made breakfast for a change. But you can grab a muffin or something before we hit the tennis court." I forced a smile. Cort tilted his head, a look of concern passing over his face. He could tell something was wrong. "I could use another cup of coffee, to be honest."

As we walked toward the entrance to the Club's restaurant,

I noticed the tennis courts were full. "Whoever's playing on our court is still grinding it out, so take your time eating."

Cortland Tyler and I were lifelong friends. We'd gone to St. Christopher's School together, as well as the University of Virginia, then Georgetown University for law school. Now he worked for Mom, and like me, he was a partner at the firm. He was the first person I told I was gay, and it turned out he was too. For a while, I thought he had a crush on me, but if he ever had, those feelings had been replaced by a friendly rivalry both on and off the tennis courts.

My family was old money, but he had even more prestige. Cort was a direct descendant of President John Tyler, and his relatives still lived at the family plantation, Sherwood Forest, in Charles City county. Though we were friends, there was a competitive streak in both of us. Neither of us liked to lose, especially at tennis. Most Saturdays we'd duke it out on the tennis courts.

"So, how is the old ball and chain?" Cort asked as soon as we sat down. Before I could answer, a server came by and took our order. As soon as coffee was in front of us, I answered.

"Carter is doing, um, okay." I sighed.

"Well, he might be doing fine, but you look horrible. What's wrong?" Cort swiped a curly lock of red hair off his forehead.

Shit. Cort knew me better than most people, and it would be impossible to put one over on him. Before I could think of the right lies to tell him, the truth came tumbling out.

"The state of Colorado fucked up, and it turns out me and Carter aren't legally married."

Cort's mouth opened, then shut.

"You know how I feel about Carter. He's my husband in my heart, even if we aren't really married." I combed my hair back with my fingers. "I talked to Mom about it, and she said to keep my mouth shut. It might benefit me in the future if things ever go bad between us."

"You mean to tell me that Carter and you aren't officially together anymore?" Cort's eyes widened.

"No, I mean, yes. Shit. I don't know where we stand. All I know is I'll do anything to..." A sweaty man in tennis gear ran up to us and we both turned our attention to him.

"Hey, are you Asher and Cort?" The man swiped at his forehead with his wristband.

"Yeah."

"Tennis court is all yours. Just had my ass handed to me by my kid." The man laughed and ran off, followed by a teenage boy. Cort drained his coffee, then stood and smirked at me.

"A hundred bucks if I win in two sets. Fifty if I win it in three." Cort stretched out his hand. I reached for it, thinking he would help me to my feet. Instead, he snatched it back and laughed. "I'm gonna kick your ass, Asher."

———

We'd split the first two sets, and it was the most competitive match we'd ever played. Normally we went for broke, especially if we were playing for cash. Cort was grunting when he hit the ball, and neither of us ever put that much effort into a tennis match. When we changed sides of the court, he snarled, "I'm kicking your ass, Yates."

But I was determined to win, so when we went to a tie-break at the end of the third set, I gritted my teeth and forced my aching legs forward. Both of us preferred playing from the baseline, so when Cort served, then raced to the net for a volley, it threw me off my game.

"Fuck." I muttered. If Cort won the next point, I'd be out fifty bucks. But it wasn't the money. Somehow, this match felt personal, like we weren't playing just to win. I'd swear Cort was determined to humiliate me.

Cort tossed the ball in the air, but his racket didn't connect. He held his hand up to apologize, then a ferocious grin spread across his cheeks. Seconds later, he tossed the ball in the air again, and with a grunt, he faked a big serve and instead hit the ball underhanded, where it landed inches away from the net on my side of the court.

"You asshole!" I yelled and scrambled for the ball. I knew there was no way I'd reach it, but my body moved on instinct. Shockingly, my racket made contact with the ball, but it went into the net. I fell on my back with a groan. What the hell was wrong with Cort? We never played using sketchy techniques. Both of us were competitive, but this was unheard of.

The racket fell from my hand and I covered my face with my hands. Then I heard footsteps running up, and Cort completed my humiliation.

"Fifty bucks, loser."

I removed my hands to behold the asshole grinning down at me. My fists clenched, and all I wanted to do was belt Cort, hit that smug smile from his face. This wasn't a friendly tennis match, at least not from my perspective. Technically, he hadn't cheated, but the way he won was looked down on by most players. What I wanted to know was why? Why was he determined to win so badly?

I reached into my pocket, pulled out my wallet, and tossed the money on the ground.

"Go fuck yourself, Cort."

———

Cort got me so riled up I ran to my car and tore out of the parking lot. Several people we knew had seen the conclusion of our match, and now that I had some distance, I was embarrassed. I never acted that way in public, much less with a friend like Cort. This situation with Carter was making me say and do things I normally wouldn't do.

When I arrived home, there wasn't a single car in the driveway, which meant the lunatics had probably gone shopping. What I wanted, no, needed, was Carter. I pulled out my phone and texted him.

> Hey babe
>
> Remember that romantic Italian place in Goochland we used to go to?

Ten minutes passed, and I texted again.

> Let's go tonight.

Half an hour later. Nothing.

> Please?

CHAPTER 6

CARTER

"Ooh, look at these antique vases." Mom gingerly picked up a pink crystal one, then flipped it over. "These are perfect, and look at the price. I already know several clients who would pay triple this amount of money without batting an eye."

"Whoever died had exceptional taste." I whispered. "Grab the entire collection, Mom."

My mother lived to shop, so we hit up these estate sales as much as possible. Even though the showroom turned a decent profit, it was nothing compared to the design portion of the business. But it kept Mom happy and gave her something to do. I'd learned from a very young age that Mom must always be busy and feel wanted. Otherwise, she cooked up drama. It was probably where I got my penchant for theatrics, though I was working on that with Belinda Therapista.

"I thought we were coming for throw pillows." Mom said, then she waved a bejeweled hand toward one of the people running the sale. "We'll take all of these. Please hold them for us since we're still browsing."

"I haven't seen any worth buying." I tilted my head toward a threadbare Italian vintage sofa, which looked to be from around 1950. There were two tasseled pillows on it that had seen better days.

"Where does Marjorie get most of her accessories?" Mom took my arm and steered me toward the stairs. We were in a Victorian era home in Crozet next door to railroad tracks. How the owners could stand the noise baffled me. "She might be a bitch, but she has excellent taste."

"Mom." I shook my head at the curse. "She's not that bad. Anyhow, most of her furnishings have been in the family for generations. You'd have to ask Asher's grandmother, Clair. Marjorie's always busy working at the law firm."

"You mean always drinking, at work, at home, wherever she can find a bottle." Mom murmured, picking up the corner of a stunning quilt. "Wow, look at the craftsmanship. Too bad our customers wouldn't like it."

"Do you like it, Mom?"

"Oh, I love it. It would be perfect for cold winter nights in front of the fireplace." Mom smoothed her hand over the red, white, and green material.

I waved at one of the workers. "We'll take this, please."

"Oh, sweety, you don't…"

"If it makes you happy, Mom, it makes me happy, too." I grinned, delighted to see Mom's face light up. "Now if I could figure out how to make Asher happy."

"Oh honey, you just keep being yourself, that's all." Mom pecked me on the cheek. "And keep your mouth shut about you-know-what."

"This is ridiculous. Lying to Asher will only backfire in the long run. Lies always do. That's why you and Dad divorced." I saw a painting of a horse and pointed at it. "You're the art expert. Look at that painting and see if it's worth anything, because we have several clients who'd pay through the nose for something like that."

"Your father lied constantly." Mom breezed by me, stopping in front of the painting. I hurried over to her. "He couldn't keep it in his pants."

"But you're encouraging me to lie, too."

"No I'm not." Mom bent down to examine the signature at the bottom corner of the canvas. Her arm shot up, waving at a worker. "We'll take this, please."

"Yes you are."

"No, it's not a lie to say nothing. Just pretend like that letter never came. If no one knows about it, it can't be true." Mom looped her arm through mine and led us toward the stairs. The home was three stories, with brilliant stained glass windows along the staircase.

"Mom, that's cheating, and you know it. Honesty is always the best."

Mom stopped in her tracks and turned to me. "If you were dealing with a normal family, I'd agree with you. But these people are abnormal. They are billionaires who live their entire lives being waited on hand and foot by that old black woman."

"Mom, Florida is family, and they treat her like gold. Like, she seriously doesn't have to work another day in her life. They fully funded her pension years ago. She stays because she loves them, and they love her." I sighed, knowing how Florida felt. When I moved to the Yates estate, I felt awkward getting used to their lifestyle. But the family embraced me with open arms, and the thought of giving them up because of an awful bureaucratic mixup made me want to chow down on all the carbs. My phone buzzed in my pocket, and when I reached for it, Mom stopped me.

"Telling the truth could mean the end of your privileged life." She whispered. "When you were a little boy, I promised myself that you'd live better than I did. Now you want to throw it all away by telling those billionaire lawyers the truth? I didn't raise you to be stupid, Carter."

———

It wasn't until we got in the car that I remembered that someone had texted me. I glanced at the screen of my phone and grinned. "Aww. Asher wants to take me to this romantic Italian restaurant in Goochland we used to go to when we were dating." I tapped out a quick message, telling him I'd meet him there after dropping Mom off at her place. Maybe things weren't as bad as I thought they were.

"What's the name of it?" Mom asked.

"Pastabilities. It's a few miles west of Short Pump Town Center on Broad Street." I grinned. "Maybe you're right Mom. At least for tonight, I won't say a word about this mess to Asher."

She patted my knee. "Mother always knows best."

———

After dropping off Mom, I raced to the restaurant, a perma-grin stretched across my cheeks. I switched on the Beyonce album we'd fallen in love with, remembering how we used to dance to it next to the river behind the Yates home. Or how we'd fool around in the abandoned boathouse by the pier.

"You were such a romantic, Asher." I sighed, then checked my reflection in the rearview mirror one last time before arriving at the restaurant. "I love you so damned much."

When I drove up, Asher was leaning against his Jaguar in the parking lot across the street from Pastabilities. He looked so dashing, wearing a casual Ben Sherman outfit I'd bought him. I loved the retro feel of the stripes, and how the sweater was molded to his muscular arms. But something felt off. Why was Asher shaking his head like that?

"Is something wrong?" I asked as I got out of the car. "You don't look thrilled to…"

Asher pointed at the restaurant.

"Oh. Wow, what happened to this place?" I muttered. What had once been a charming eatery now appeared to be on its last legs. The restaurant was in an old, white plantation house. There used to be tables and giant ferns on the large patio out front where we'd drink wine. Now they were gone. When we first started dating, we'd come here because none of our friends or family knew about it, and we could be alone. Glancing down at my feet, there was garbage strewn across the parking lot.

"Do you think it's still open?" Asher asked. "There's only two other cars in the lot."

One of them was a beat-up Volkswagen Beetle, with patches of rust dotting the exterior. The other was an ancient pickup truck with hippy bumper stickers. Peace signs, and hearts.

"Let's go somewhere else, Carter. This isn't anything like the place we used to love." Asher put his hands on my shoulders and pecked my cheek. "We could head downtown and hang out in Shockoe Slip."

"No." I took his hand, and we crossed the street. "It might be a little rundown, but maybe the inside is better." We needed to reconnect, because the last few days had been hellish. I wanted our romance back, and maybe coming to Pastabilities was the way to do it.

"Whatever you want, sweetheart."

A minute later, we pushed open the entrance, and both of us gasped. A sign was strung up over the hostess station saying it was under new management. It was partially ripped, and a layer of dust sat on every available surface. There was nobody inside, or at least that's what we thought. Somebody coughed, and Asher yelled out, "Is there anyone here?"

An old man shuffled out and looked shocked to see us.

"We used to come here a few years ago and eat at a table on the patio." I forced a grin on my face. "Would it be possible to put one out there? We'd love to..." I began, and the man cut me off.

"We don't do that anymore." He said, and I noticed a gravy stain on his white shirt.

"If I pay you an extra $50, would you mind moving a table outside?" Asher asked, and the man's eyes lit up.

"No problem, sir. Lorrie!" The man called out. A skinny older woman who looked like she'd gone to Woodstock in the sixties and never recovered from the experience, strolled out. She was wearing love beads around her neck, and her straight white hair hung to her waist. "Yeah, Bubba?"

"Help me move a table out on the patio. Oh, and bring some candles. It's getting dark outside and the bulbs blew out a few days ago." The man ordered, and the woman scowled. So much for peace, love, and understanding. A few minutes later, the woman seated us, lighting a multi-colored candle with wax dripping down the sides. She placed menus in front of us then hurried away.

"Well, this was unexpected." Asher winked. "But let's make the best of it, unless you want to go somewhere else?"

"No, this is fine." I muttered, dread washing through me. A moment later, four motorcycles parked across the street. Asher reached out to take my hand, but one glance at the bikers heading our way made him withdraw it. No use provoking the rednecks. Their leather jackets were covered in rebel flags, and one of the guys had a bump under his lip. Probably chewing tobacco.

It occurred to me that this restaurant, a place we used to

love, had changed, and it would never be the same again. What had once been charming, and sweet, was now cheap and tawdry. No, the better word was decayed. This place was dying a slow death, like our relationship.

"Fuck it." I reached into my jacket pocket and pulled out the letter from Colorado. Maybe the only way to save our relationship was to ignore Mom, and be upfront and honest about this whole mess. My hand trembled as I handed it to him. "A courier delivered this to my office."

Asher's face lost all color.

"Read it."

CHAPTER 7
ASHER

Why hadn't my mother and I realized the state of Colorado would send Carter the same notice they'd sent me? We were supposedly the top law firm in the entire state, and we'd been stupidly naïve. Actually, I hadn't been naïve, I'd been self-centered, only thinking of myself. Of course they'd sent him the notice.

"Go on, read it, Asher." Carter's hands shook as he held out the letter. Reluctantly, I slid it out of his fingers and scanned the page. It was the exact same notice they'd sent me, except for our names.

"Um, well…"

"I can't believe this!" Carter yelled, and the hippy waitress ran outside.

"Are you guys cool?" She asked, her straight gray hair now held back in a ponytail.

"Booze." Carter said. "We need lots of booze."

"Do you have a wine menu?" I asked, and the woman looked at me as if I'd just asked for a plate of freshly poached infants.

"We've got beer, and, oh yeah. There's that bottle of chianti we…"

"We'll take the wine, thanks." Carter waved his hand dismissively toward her and she left.

"Carter, this isn't a total disaster. We were having a new ceremony, and instead of just repeating our vows, we'll get a marriage license and make it legal." My hands were in my lap, and I crossed my fingers, hoping he wouldn't freak out too badly. Carter opened his mouth to speak, but I held a hand up. "Baby, you can go hog wild with the ceremony, and I won't say a word. Anything you want, is yours. New Dior suits, the caterers of your choice, and we'll throw the biggest wedding reception the Country Club has ever seen."

Carter glanced up to the darkening sky. "Are you being serious? Because if you're saying this to…"

"Here's your chianti." The waitress interrupted, placing an enormous jug of red wine between us. "Do you know what you'd like to eat?"

"You haven't given us menus yet." Carter smiled sweetly at her. "Nor wine glasses."

"Oh, dude, sorry." The woman raced back inside.

"Carter, I love you so much. All I want is for you to be happy, and if that means an enormous wedding, then so be it." I sighed, forcing myself not to think of the expense. Most folks thought wealthy people spent their money. My parents taught me the opposite. In order to build wealth, you were frugal, made the right investments, and were fortunate enough to be born to rich parents.

"Here you are fellas." The waitress placed the menus and glasses in front of us. "I'll give you a few minutes to look things over." She drawled, then slunk back inside.

Carter opened the menu, then shut it and pulled out his phone. A moment later he handed it to me, a huge grin spreading across his cheeks. "Here are the suits. I found them on the Dior website. You will look so handsome wearing it."

The suit was perfect, if you were Elton John, that was. Glitter, feathers, and matching black felt hats. But, Carter had exceptional taste and must have seen something in these garish outfits that I didn't.

"Honey, when I got that letter from Colorado, I was terrified you'd have a meltdown." I reached across the table and laid my hand on Carter's. "But you see, everything is turning out for the best. You wanted to have a proper wedding, and now we're having one. And these suits are, well, indescribable."

Carter eyed me for a moment, then snatched his hand back from mine. "Wait. You got one of these awful letters too?"

"Well…"

"When were you going to tell me about it?" Carter crossed his arms over his chest and glared at me.

"I um.."

"Just as I thought. You were pretending like everything was just peachy, hoping I'd never find out. And I know why, too." Carter's eyes narrowed. "You never wanted to be married in the first place, and this…" He jabbed his finger onto the open letter between us. "…was your dream come true." Carter got to his feet, and my heart missed a beat. What the hell was wrong now? He was getting everything he wanted, but for some reason was shifting blame to me. Carter swiped at his eyes. "So this is it, huh? Now we're suddenly single. At least we don't have to bother with a messy divorce." He spun around and raced across the street to the parking lot.

"Hey!" I leapt to my feet. "Where are you going?"

He froze, but didn't turn around. Carter's shoulders straightened, then he slowly got in his car, slamming the door shut. The waitress returned. "Do you know what you'd…"

Carter's wheels spun in the gravel, and a moment later he

was gone, taking my heart with him. I glanced up at the wait-ress, her head tilted and her lips pursed.

"Nothing. I'll pay for the wine, and sorry about, well, every-thing." I sighed, my eyes never leaving the fading taillights of Carter's car.

———

When I drove past the main house most of the lights were off. "Where on earth is…oh yeah. Mom's on a date with the judge." At least someone's love life was taking off. Carter's car wasn't there, and I prayed he was at the cottage.

A minute later, I parked in front of my dark house. Carter's car wasn't there, and I prayed he was all right. When Carter had fled the restaurant, I'd been tempted to call or text him. But I realized he probably needed some space, so I'd taken the long way home. What I hadn't expected was for him not to be here. Where the hell was he?

When I got out of the car, I heard a crash coming from the back shed where we kept the trash cans. My heart raced, and I was halfway to the shed before I realized I didn't have a weapon. What if it was a burglar, or worse? I let myself into the house, grabbed a knife out of the butcher block, then switched on all the outdoor lights. When I opened the backdoor, the little thief eyed me for a moment, then scampered off, leaving garbage in his wake.

"Fucking trash panda." I sighed, then I sank to the ground next to the door. The knife fell from my hand as the first sob tore through my chest. Damn it, I loved Carter, but thanks to taking Mom's advice, I'd made a mess of everything.

"Where are you? Please, Jesus, let him be okay."

CHAPTER 8

CARTER

Carytown was hopping as I drove through it. A line snaked around the corner from Babes, the local lesbian bar. Since it was Saturday night, it meant the drag kings and queens were hitting the stage. I used to go there occasionally before I met Asher, preferring the relative calm of being one of the few guys in a girl bar over hitting the gay bars. I always felt like a piece of meat at Thirsty's and Barcode. When you walked into a boy bar, every man sized you up in not-so-subtle ways that creeped me out.

Since I was a child, I'd always fantasized about meeting my perfect match, getting married, and spending the rest of my life with him. Despite my outward appearance, I was very old-fashioned, and had never slept around. What I lived for was romance, nights spent in front of a roaring fireplace drinking wine, or being with friends and family.

"God, I miss the Yates." I sighed, then pulled into the parking lot of my building. Despite the salon and my business being closed, the parking lot was nearly full thanks to partiers.

They ignored the no parking after hours sign, and frankly, I didn't have the energy to have all these cars towed.

I popped open the trunk, then got out of the car to get my overnight bag. After leaving Asher at that tragic restaurant, I'd raced home. Shit, I mean Asher's home, and threw a few things in an overnight bag. It was just enough clothes to last a few days, so I could figure out my next move. After shutting the trunk, I looked up to the top floor of the old church.

"Welcome to your new home." I forced my feet forward until I was climbing up the back steps. Before I married Asher, well, before I thought I was married, I'd lived in the loft on the top floor. It was a little cramped compared to the cottage we'd shared, but it would have to do for now.

I hadn't set foot in the old loft in years. Mom recommended that I rent it out, but something always held me back. The thought of a stranger having access to the building when I wasn't there turned me off. But maybe it had been a premonition of some sort. Like, I knew that one day I'd be back, living over my shop.

"Home sweet home." I sighed, unlocking the door. When I switched on the lights, I could see a thick layer of dust covering everything. "I'd better call Florida and ask her if she knows an excellent maid." There was no way I'd let Corinne work for both me and Asher. I didn't want her reporting anything to Asher, and I was positive he'd pump her for information.

"Damn it, I feel like I'm getting divorced, and I was never fucking married to begin with." I threw my bag on the couch and sank onto the cushions next to it. A puff of dust surrounded me, and I waved it away and coughed. Every cell in my body felt heavy, like there was a toxic sludge traveling through my veins instead of blood.

"There's no way I'm falling asleep without help." I sighed, then opened my bag and fished out a bottle of Benadryl. "I love you, Asher." After shaking three tablets into my hand, I pushed myself off the couch and went to the tiny kitchen for water.

I turned on the overhead light, opened the cabinet over the sink, and recoiled. The few glasses I had were covered in dust. When I pulled one out, small dark pellets fell to the counter, and I jumped back.

"Shit. Fucking mice." I shuddered. "Just a few hours ago, I lived on a grand estate. Now I live in a rodent infested apartment." I turned on the water, and for a moment the water came out a mud brown color before turning clear. I rinsed the dust off the glass, filled it, then popped the pills.

———

"Where am I?"

My eyes fluttered open, and I reached for Asher, but found only a pillow. "Damn it." I sighed, then reached over to the nightstand and grabbed my phone. It was nearly noon. I hadn't slept this much in years, yet I still felt exhausted. There was a string of texts from Asher, and I reluctantly read the first one.

> Where are you?

"Alone," I muttered, then tapped on the next message.

> Please let me know you are safe

I noticed the time he'd sent it. Two in the morning. Pressure built behind my eyes. Asher was genuinely worried. I glanced through the rest of them, and they were all the same. He sent the last message at six in the morning.

"Jesus, I hope he got some sleep." I decided to text him a message, letting him know I was okay.

I am safe. Please don't contact me unless it's an emergency.

I hit send, then stared up at the ceiling. Cobwebs were in every corner, and if I didn't get this place cleaned up soon, I'd have an asthma attack from all the dust and mice turds.

My phone pinged, and it fell to my lap. When I picked it up, I noticed my knuckles were red, and cracked. It was like my body was aging overnight from all the stress of the last few days. Mom had warned me to keep my mouth shut, that I'd lose everything if I told the truth. Looked like she was right, but I still felt like I'd done the right thing. Keeping the truth from Asher was wrong, which was why I was livid with him. He'd known all along, and I wondered if he'd have gone to his grave never telling me the truth about our marriage.

"Was our entire relationship based on lies? What else has Asher kept from me?" I shook my head, then looked at the latest message.

Thank God you're okay. Come home.

———

"Where are you Carter?" Florida sounded pissed. I'd spent the last couple of hours trying to clean the place up, but I needed professional help. I was about to call her, but she beat me to it. "What the hell has your man done to you?"

"How do you...?"

"Asher didn't sleep all night, and Mrs. Yates stayed up with him." Poor Asher, he should have taken pills like I did.

"Where is he now?"

"He went to the cottage an hour ago, hopefully to sleep." Florida said. "When are you coming home?"

"I'm at my new home." I sighed. "We're not married anymore, Florida." I sighed. "He knew we weren't married, yet he said nothing."

"I don't understand."

In my head I could see Florida in the kitchen of the Yates' estate, wringing her hands. "When we got married in Colorado, there was a mistake, a technical glitch. Turns out our marriage has never been valid, and Asher knew about it."

"I'm going to smack that boy into next week!" Florida yelled, and a small smile spread across my cheeks. At least someone cared about me. "How did you find out?"

"The state of Colorado sent both of us a letter stating that the marriage wasn't valid." My stomach growled, and I realized I hadn't eaten since yesterday. If I was with Asher, I'd just stroll up the driveway and get Florida to make something for me. "I told Asher about it, and it turns out he knew too, but was keeping me in the dark."

"Jesus Christ Almighty. Well, I can tell you right now that Asher loves you. He and his momma were up all night." Florida clucked her tongue. "I wonder if Mrs. Yates knows about the marriage? She's worried about you, too."

"I don't know." I sat down on the couch and coughed from the dust. "Florida, do you know anyone who could clean my place part-time? It's too small for a full-time maid, but to be honest, it's a disaster right now."

"What about Corinne? She knows you, and…"

"I don't want your niece to work for me because she works for Asher, too. Don't you know anyone else?" Honestly, I'd do it myself, but I didn't have experience dealing with mice and years of neglect. This loft used to be stunning, and now it was a shambles. Like my life.

"My sister Georgia might do it. She's retired, but money is money. If it's just part-time, I bet she'd help you out."

"Good lord, do you have a sister named South Carolina, too?" I grinned at my stupid joke.

"Shut up, Carter." I heard a smile in Florida's voice, then a door slammed in the background.

"Is that Carter?" It was Asher. He must have just come into the kitchen. A tear snaked down the side of my nose and I brushed it away.

"I've gotta go." I said. "Give your sister my number and tell her to call me ASAP. I've got mice, and the place is a disaster."

"It's him, isn't it." I heard Asher's voice again. "Let me talk to him, Florida."

"Don't touch my phone. Carter doesn't want to talk…"

"Carter, please!" Asher must have snatched the phone out of Florida's hand. God, I loved this man so much, but there was only so much I could take. Maybe we could work it out, but I kept remembering him saying that he wished we'd never been married in the first place. "Baby, I love you."

My breath hitched, and without a second thought, I disconnected the call.

CHAPTER 9

ASHER

"Give me that damned phone!" Florida snatched the phone back from me and scowled. "Carter? Are you still there?" Florida shook her head in disgust and placed the phone on the kitchen counter. "You've broken Carter's heart, Asher. Shame on you!"

"Why is everyone blaming me?" I went to the pantry and found Mom's special sauce, then went back in the kitchen and poured myself a well-deserved vodka on the rocks. I nearly choked on the first sip because my throat was so tight. Florida just stared at me, the judgment apparent in her eyes. "Stop it." I snapped.

"What?" Florida crossed her arms over her chest.

"Judging me. Good God, you've known me my entire life and you always take Carter's side over mine." I drank the rest of the vodka and slammed the tumbler on the counter. "What do I have to do to make you understand this situation isn't my fault?"

"Who's fault is it?" Florida said, then poked me in the chest. "You're the one who said you didn't want to be married to

Carter. I've got eyes and ears, boy, so don't act all innocent with me."

I opened my mouth, but nothing would come out. Damn it, she was right. Suddenly, a strange smell was in the air. Both Florida and I sniffed, then turned toward the door. Mary Jane and Granny were standing in the doorway with gunk in their hair. They must be touching up their roots.

"Whenever Lila Brooke and I argue, I just leave her be until she calms down. You might try the same approach, dear." Mary Jane grinned, while Granny shook her head at me.

"Bless his heart," Granny pointed at me. "Asher can't understand why Carter is angry. Child, what do you expect Carter to feel? You tell him in front of the entire family that you don't want to be married, and then you find out you aren't. Of course, Carter's feelings are hurt, and I don't blame him one bit. He feels abandoned."

"Amen to that." Florida picked up her phone and placed a call. "Georgia? It's me, Florida. I need your help with something." She walked out of the room.

Mary Jane opened the refrigerator and pulled out a plate of cookies.

"May I remind you that Carter abandoned me. Are those for real, or edibles?" I pointed at the cookies.

"They aren't laced, if that's what you mean." She pulled the plastic wrap off and handed me and Granny a cookie. "Though you could probably use something a little stronger to take the edge off."

"I'm surprised none of us have been to rehab yet." I bit into the cookie and smiled. Peanut butter cookies were my favorite.

"Unlike regular people, we don't hide our guilty pleasures." Mary Jane spun around and winked. "We celebrate them!"

"Do we ever." Granny strolled into the pantry and came back with Mom's vodka. "How much longer before we rinse,

Mary Jane?" She pointed at her hair. Granny kept hers platinum blonde, while Mary Jane's was a more natural looking light brown. Because the hair dye was only on the roots, both looked like they'd stuck their fingers in electrical sockets.

"About fifteen more minutes."

"Want a top up, Asher?" Granny filled a tumbler and pointed at mine. I placed my hand on top of it and shook my head no. The simple thing to do would be to drink until I passed out and ignore my problems. But I knew it would more likely accomplish the opposite, and I'd hyper-focus on Carter until I was a hot mess.

"Darlings." Mom swept into the kitchen, wearing a pink silk robe, with enormous curlers in her hair. She grabbed the vodka, poured herself a tumbler, then put it back in the pantry. "My date with Judge Gottwald was so marvelous we're meeting for tea this afternoon."

"Glad one of us has a decent love life." I muttered, then grabbed a bottle of water out of the fridge.

"Have you heard from Carter?" Mom asked. Her gaze met mine, then she grimaced. "That bad, huh?"

"Yes, it's a disaster." I sat on a stool and brushed a tear away. I'd swear my tear ducts were attached to my bladder, because they wouldn't stop. "Who knows where he is?."

"Why? Why can't you fix this?" Mom sat next to me and rubbed between my shoulder blades.

"We were so stupid, Mom. The state of Colorado sent him the exact same letter they sent me. Then he figured out that I'd known about our marriage not being valid, and he went ballistic. Florida is the only person who knows where Carter is, and she won't tell me." I said, then Granny and Mary Jane sat down next to us.

"I dye my hair too, but I still hate that smell." Mom waved her hand in front of her face. "Darling, I think both of you are being childish." She patted my knee. "You agreed to marry him again, and now Carter's having another hissy fit."

"If he hadn't said that he wished he never married Carter, Asher wouldn't be in the doghouse." Granny pointed at me. "Child, you'd better be prepared to grovel, because I suspect Carter won't accept a simple apology."

"I'll do anything, I swear."

Mom grabbed a napkin and blotted my cheeks.

"I've told him I love him, and that I'll marry him again. Hell, I even told him he could have the biggest, grandest wedding of the century, and he's still angry."

"Where is Carter?" Mom pointed at Florida, who'd just walked back into the kitchen.

"I'm not telling." She leaned against the wall opposite us and crossed her arms over her chest. "Carter made me promise to keep my mouth shut."

Mom sighed dramatically. "You're not helping the situation, Florida. Do you want to see the boys back together, or do you want them miserable?"

"It's Asher's fault."

"Florida, you don't know the full story. If I were a judge in a courtroom, I'd toss the case out due to stupidity on both their parts. My wonderful son occasionally sticks his foot in his mouth, and Carter is having a complete breakdown, drama-queen style." Mom stood, then crossed over to Florida and placed her hands on her shoulders. "Now tell me. Where is Carter?"

"He's living over his shop in that old church." Florida rolled her eyes. "Said he's got mice."

"Well, that takes care of one question." Mom turned to me. "Now that you know where to find him, what are you going to do to win him back?"

"I'm going to him, now." I leapt to my feet and raced for the door.

"Wait!" Florida yelled.

"What?"

"He doesn't want to see you." Florida's lips twisted. "Plus, he'll kill me if he knows I told you."

"Then I'll see you at your funeral, because nothing is stopping me from getting Carter back."

———

I parked my car next to Carter's Mercedes, switched off the engine, and froze. Everything seemed sped up, and my heart was pounding. What if Florida was right? Would Carter flip out if I show up on his doorstep?

"Yes, and he'll probably flip out if I don't at least attempt to talk to him face to face." I leaned my forehead against the steering wheel and sighed. "The love of my life is acting like a fool, and so am I. How the hell did things get so bad between us?"

If I were being honest with myself, I'd realize that this latest blowup was a long time coming. Mom was right, Carter was a drama queen, and sometimes I spoke the truth when a little white lie would be better. When I confessed that I sometimes wish we hadn't got married, I should have said nothing, or said, yes dear, of course I want to be married to you. Because most of the time I did. Like right now, I really wanted my husband back.

"Doesn't every married couple go through ups and downs?" I glanced up at the roof of the old church. There weren't any windows in that small apartment, and I didn't know how Carter could stand living there. "We'd had an argument the night before, and at that time I didn't want to be married. Ask any married person after an argument, and they'd probably say they didn't want to be hitched, either."

I got out of the car and trudged toward the back stairs. When I got to the back entrance, I raised my fist to knock and froze. Sweat dripped down my sides, and for the first time in a very long time, I felt truly afraid. Afraid that Carter no longer wanted me, and that he didn't want us to be married ever again.

"Would that be so bad? Maybe we could live in... who am I kidding? The only man I want is inside this building, and the only way to get him back is to fucking grovel like Granny said."

I knocked on the door, then noticed the doorbell and pushed it. I knew his loft was on the third floor, so I expected him to be a minute or two. Finally, I heard footsteps approach, and the door flew open.

"Who are you?" I asked. A heavy-set woman with waist-length gray braids stood there with her hands on her hips, shaking her head at me and scowling.

"Mr. Camden doesn't want to see you."

"You mean Mr. Yates, he..."

"I've been told that you aren't allowed inside the building. Now, if you'll excuse me, I have to get back to work." The woman slammed the door in my face.

"Jesus." I leaned against the railing and slumped. How the hell could I make things right when Carter wouldn't even see me? And who the hell was that woman?

"Fuck it. If Carter won't see me, maybe he'll talk to someone else." I pulled my phone out and searched my contacts until I found the right number. He answered after three rings.

"Hey Asher. What's up?"

"Cort, I desperately need your help. Can we meet at the club for a drink?"

CHAPTER 10

ASHER

"Not up for a match, Asher?" Cort asked as we settled into our seats. We were at the country club, and the dark, wood-paneled walls accurately reflected my mood.

"No, sorry." I muttered, stirring my drink. "I've asked you here today for help."

"Is it one of your cases? Because..." Cort squinted his eyes.

"No, it's nothing work-related. Remember what we talked about, you know, about me and Carter?" I glanced around the room and noticed we were the only people here, which was odd for a Sunday.

"You mentioned that you and Carter are no longer married, or you never were I believe." Cort grinned. "How am I supposed to help?"

"Carter won't speak to me, and I was hoping you could help me get through to him." I sighed, and the back of my head felt tight. Hopefully, I wasn't getting a headache.

"I'm confused, Asher. What exactly is going on? Does he not

want to marry you again?" Cort sipped his drink, eyeing me curiously.

"He won't talk, damn it. I've told him already that I want us to be married again, that it would be the wedding of his dreams. Hell, I'll do anything to get him back." I drained my drink while Cort steepled his hands under his chin. "He moved out of the house and is living over his design shop in Carytown."

"He what?" Cort's eyes widened.

"Yes, he left me. And I need your help to get him back." The waitress came by with a fresh drink and took my empty glass away.

"Well, Asher, I'm not sure how I can be of help to you. I mean, I like Carter okay, but we're hardly good friends. We probably would never have met if it weren't for you. Though I have to admit, I've always been a little jealous." Cort raked his fingers through his thick red hair.

"Jealous? What on earth are you jealous of?" I said, rubbing my chin.

"Well, Carter. He might not come from our social background, but he's a very attractive man. Actually, that's probably why I've always liked your husb... I mean your ex-husband, I guess. Because he's different, and refreshing to be around."

Now it was my turn to be jealous. Cort had never once mentioned to me that he had the hots for Carter. It was understandable, of course. When I first met Carter, that was what I thought, too. Everyone in my social set was very stuffy, to say the least. When I was around Carter, I felt freed from the silly rules and behaviors of my preppy friends. I daresay that was why my family fell in love with Carter, too.

"Look, he doesn't want to see me. But maybe he'd speak to you, Cort."

"Are you sure you want me to get involved? Because I've

never had a serious relationship in my life. I'm not sure I'd even know what to say." Cort signaled the waitress for another drink.

"Honestly, I don't know who to turn to. Please, Cort? Will you talk to Carter for me?"

———

Monday morning was pure, unadulterated hell. After leaving Cort at the country club, I'd gone home and had a few more drinks with the girls. By the time Mom got back from her date with the judge, we were all three sheets to the wind, and a pounding head was my payment for a few hours of forget-fulness.

Now I faced a growing pile of paperwork, and a secretary who also woke up on the wrong side of the bed. All I wanted was to go home and find Carter in bed waiting for me. Since the chances of that happening were slim to none, I felt helpless.

When I came into the office this morning, I'd gone to Cort's office and again, I urged him to help me with Carter. He said he'd talk to him sometime today, so I was keeping my fingers crossed it would help.

"Knock, knock."

I glanced up to see Mom standing in the doorway of my office. "Where's my secretary?"

"Not at her desk. That's why I'm barging in unannounced." Mom sat across from me and smiled. "Have you heard anything from Carter?"

"No. He won't speak to me, so I've roped Cort into helping out." I said, then Mom handed me a folder with more paper-work. "Mom, I've billed more hours than any other partner in the firm the last couple of months, and I'd…"

"I'm so proud of you, dear." Mom stood, walked to the

mini-bar by the window, and helped herself to a drink. "When I die, the family business will be in excellent hands."

"Oh mother, don't even talk about…"

"Darling, it's true, just a fact of life. I don't expect to kick the bucket anytime soon. But I'm prepared to meet my maker." Mom sat down and winked. "Let's just hope he's prepared to meet me."

"Mom, the reason I bring up my billable hours is if I can persuade Carter to remarry me, I'd like to take some time off. Perhaps a month or two. I need quality time with Carter, so we can work through our problems."

"Of which you have many." Mom said. "If you can win Carter back, and trust me, the whole family is rooting for you, I'll give you all the time off you need. We'll just spread your casework out to some associates, though you might have to do a little teleworking."

"That's not a problem." I put my face in my hands and sighed. "Cort said he'd help by talking to Carter, since he's not speaking to me."

"Are you sure about that? I mean, Cort is a friend, but perhaps you should keep this problem in the family. You know how people gossip." Mom tossed her drink back and stood. "Honey, you need to go to Carter yourself, and beg, no, not beg, grovel. If you hadn't told him you didn't wish to be married, this situation would never have gotten out of hand." Mom tilted her head and pointed at me.

"What?"

"Get out of here." Mom came behind the desk and leaned over me. She punched the off button on my computer, then shut the open files. "Go to Carter and take care of this now. Are you due in court today?"

"No, I don't have a courtroom case until next week. Most of my work is about taxes, and…"

"Asher, I'm ordering you to leave. Stop this tragedy from getting any worse."

———

Instead of parking in the lot of Carter's building, I parked a block away at the Cary Court shopping center. This way, he wouldn't see my car and run away. Since it was a Monday afternoon, there weren't too many people out and about, and hopefully Carter wouldn't be busy with a customer. When I arrived at his building, I winced.

A worker was removing the name Yates from the sign, and now it was just Camden Interiors.

"What the actual hell?" I knew his business benefitted from my family's name, so if he'd already taken my name off the sign, he must be determined to end it. My shoulders slumped, and with heavy limbs, I trudged up the concrete steps of the old church.

When I stepped inside, the little bell rang. Carter's mom Sissy stepped into the showroom, threw her arms open, and hugged me.

"Oh Asher, I'm so sorry about what's happening. I've told Carter repeatedly that he's making a serious mistake. Why can't you boys just work things out?" She kissed my cheek and stepped back. Then she glanced behind her and shook her head. "Actually, you've come at a terrible time, Asher. Um, we're um, ah…"

"So it's a date then!" I heard a familiar voice coming from the back of the store. Sissy grabbed my arm and started dragging me back to the door.

"Wait, wait, I came here to see Carter. What the hell is going on?" I pried her hands off me, then raced to the back of the store where his office was located. A second later, Carter came into view. His mouth opened and shut, then he grinned a toothy smile and rushed forward.

"Please leave." He crossed his arms over his chest.

"Carter, I just want to... Oh good, Cort is here." My friend emerged from his office, his cheeks nearly matching the color of his red hair. Carter's eyes widened, and his tan skin paled.

"So, I'll pick you up tomorrow evening at seven." Cort mumbled, then he pecked Carter on the cheek and ran past me through the exit.

"What, what the hell was that?" I couldn't believe my eyes.

"It's none of your business, but if the only way to get you to leave is telling you the truth, so be it." Carter crossed the room and stood next to Sissy. "Cort asked me on a date, and I've accepted."

CHAPTER 11

CARTER

Asher's shoulders slumped, and his eyes grew wet. Even though we weren't married now, that didn't mean I enjoyed seeing him in pain. But we had to get on with our lives, and I wasn't spending the rest of mine with someone who'd told me he wished we'd never married.

He opened his mouth, then shut it. Asher slowly turned around and headed toward the door. Heat raced through my body. How dared Asher waltz into my shop, then turn around and leave without... a fight? Was that what I wanted?

"Don't." Mom grabbed my arm. "Let him go. Can't you see he's in agony?"

"Oh, and how do you think I'm feeling? He comes to my place of business, when I've told him I want to be left alone. If he'd never said those hurtful things to me, none of this would be happening. It's Asher's fault, and as far as I'm concerned, he hasn't suffered enough." I shrugged off Mom's hand and raced for the door. When I opened it, Asher was halfway down the steps.

"We're not married, and I can go out with anyone I want." I

called down to him. Asher spun around, and my gut clenched at the sight of him. Tears were streaming down his pink cheeks, and my first instinct was to take him in my arms and kiss them away.

"I don't know what else I can do to prove my love to you." Asher put his face in his hands for a long moment, and I noticed Karina's apprentices staring at us from the parking lot. Actually, quite a few people were watching from the sidewalk too. "I agreed to another marriage, which is what I thought you wanted." Asher dropped to his knees on the sidewalk and winced. "I'll get down on my knees and ask again. What else can I do?"

"You're making a scene." I muttered, then realized we both were. All of our disagreements and dramas were both our faults, though it was easier to blame him than accept the truth. Maybe we just weren't meant to be.

Asher cupped his hands around his mouth and screamed, "I love you, Carter Camden! Marry me again!"

"Boys, what's going on out here?" I felt a hand on my shoulder and saw my hairdresser, Karina. Her heavily made-up eyes squinted at me. "This is terrible for business, Carter."

"Fuck this shit." Asher got to his feet, brushing dirt off of his knees. Several older women with curlers and foils in their hair had followed Karina outside, and they gasped at his language. "Mind your own fucking business!" Asher flipped the ladies off, and they all raced back to the salon.

"Asher, sweetie, don't behave like this on the street." Karina shook her head at him. She cut everyone's hair in the Yates clan. Karina took a step toward him, but he held up his hand.

"If you go on a date with Cort, or anyone else, then it is over between us, Carter. I love you, but I'm not a masochist." He took a few steps down the sidewalk, then turned and laughed. "Fuck that, I already AM a masochist, putting up with this bullshit for years. You and your dramas can go straight to hell."

Cort's Porsche pulled up as he was leaving. A window rolled down and with a smile he called out to me, "I'll pick you up tomorrow night at seven!"

When I strolled back into the showroom, Mom grabbed my arm and spun me around. "You are making the biggest mistake of your life." Her nostrils flared, and I flinched. Mom rarely got angry with me, and now I felt like I was seven years old again, and she was forcing me to clean my room.

"After all the things he said to me, you're taking his side?" I yanked my arm out of her grasp.

"Yes, I am." Mom shook her fist. "He's made his love for you perfectly clear, and all you're doing is throwing it away. I hate them, but the Yates family are powerful, and they love you. Like… like, I can't even wrap my head around…"

"Then don't." I stalked back toward my office with Mom on my heels. When I got to the door, I turned and faced her. "Mother, I want to get on with my life. Asher knew I didn't want him here, and…"

"He had no other choice except to come to you. Jesus, Carter. I raised you to be a smart and resourceful man, but you're acting stupid. And that man who asked you out? I've seen him at various Yates family functions. Why on earth would you agree to go out with him? You're not only pissing off Asher, but you'll alienate the rest of his family, too." Mom's shoulders sagged. "Honey, I can't tell you what to do, but maybe you should go talk to your therapist about this. Obviously you aren't listening to me. Perhaps she could help."

Belinda Therapista's office was three blocks away on Auburn Avenue. We didn't have regular therapy sessions, but she always squeezed me in whenever I called. We'd worked out a deal where I got free sessions in exchange for my design services. So far, I'd created a home office and expanded a closet for her.

Her real name was Dr. Belinda Johnson, and she was a child psychologist. We'd met at a party a few years ago, and despite her working with children, we clicked. She also bore a striking resemblance to the most fabulous supermodel of all time, Linda Evangelista. She was gorgeous, had a chic wardrobe, and most of the country club set sent their kids to her.

I'd been sitting in the waiting room for twenty long minutes. Normally I didn't feel nervous with her, but today was different. My throat felt tight, my mouth was dry, and I'd swear I was on the verge of a heart attack.

"Dr. Johnson will see you now." The motherly receptionist smiled and gestured toward Belinda's office door. My legs shook as I stood up, then I took a deep breath and walked into her office.

"Hello, Carter," she waved her manicured fingers toward the wingback leather chair in front of her desk. It was an antique I'd found at an estate sale and given to her as a gift. I settled in, then gazed at her. She tapped her nails on the desk a few times, then flashed that glittery white smile at me. If I were into women, she'd be at the top of my list. "So, how are things?"

I sighed, opened my mouth, and nothing came out.

"Oh." Therapista pursed her lips, then opened one of her desk drawers. "I think you need to talk to our old friend, Cracker." A moment later, the familiar face of her hand puppet slid onto her fingers and faced me. Damn it, I felt stupid talking to the puppet, but it really did work. Something about the bright red yarn on its head, and the purple and orange striped shirt made me open up in ways nothing else could. Perhaps it was the sing-song voice Therapista used for it? "Hi, Carter!"

I cleared my throat. "Hello, Cracker."

"Now, I want you to take five deep breaths and clear your mind." The puppet squeaked. This was a technique Therapista had taught me to focus. I was supposed to do this every day, but rarely remembered. I placed my hands on my lap, shut my eyes, and began taking deep breaths. Like always, it worked, and I felt my shoulders relax.

"Very good, Carter. The last time you were here, you were having problems with Asher."

"Yes. Cracker, I love Asher. I really, really do. But he told me he wished he'd never married me, so I left him." I swiped at my cheeks, and Therapista pushed a box of tissues across the desk with her free hand.

"You know it's okay to cry, don't you?" Cracker asked, and I snatched a tissue out of the box and mopped up my face. "This is a safe space for when you're going through bad stuff."

"Well, it's even worse than I imagined." My voice broke. I gripped my thighs and began taking deep breaths again. Finally, I blurted out, "The state of Colorado made a mistake, and it turns out Asher and I are not legally married."

Cracker gasped.

"So I left him. He'd already said he didn't want to be married, so his wish came true." I grabbed another tissue.

Cracker's red yarn hair seemed to stand up straighter. "Didn't you say you really, really love him?"

"Uh, huh." A sob tore through me.

"How do you feel about living on your own? Away from the man you love?"

"I ha-ha-hate it." The dam burst, and tears streamed from my eyes. "I want him back, but every time I see him, this red fiery ball of anger twists in my stomach." My eyes shut, and I began breathing deeply, hoping to calm the tears. "He doesn't love me the way I want him to love me." I hiccuped on the last word.

"Emily, bring Carter a bottle of Perrier, please." I heard Belinda say in her normal voice. A moment later, the receptionist walked in, placed the bottle on the desk in front of me and left.

"A long drink of water will make you feel better. Like a liquid hug!" Cracker said, so I opened my eyes and took the bottle from her desk. "Often we get cranky when we're dehydrated."

I put the bottle down and felt calm again. Therapista and Cracker always chilled me out when I felt like life was spinning out of control. "More than anything, I'd like to work things out with Asher. He even said he'd marry me again in a big ceremony at the country club. But I did something stupid."

"There's nothing stupid when you're hurting. Sometimes we lash out because we feel like our life is out of control. Your feelings are valid, little Carter." Cracker tilted on Therapista's hand, and his black and white wobbly eyes spun for a second. "So, what did you do that you feel is stupid?"

"It was totally unexpected." I still couldn't believe it. "Asher's best friend Cort came to the shop and asked me out on a date. I've never thought about him romantically. In fact, he's not my type at all. He reeks of..."

"Do you mean Cort Tyler?" Cracker asked. I nodded, and the puppet did a double take. "The Tylers are a really big deal."

"Yes, but that doesn't matter to me. What matters is that I feel nothing for him. He was always just this guy Asher worked and played tennis with. But, when he invited me to dinner, I said yes because I thought I needed to get on with my life. Asher found out, and, oh my God, we had a fight in front of my shop, right on Cary Street."

"Aww, poor Carter. Fighting is hard on the heart. You know, if you don't want to go on a date with Cort, you don't have to."

"Oh." I muttered and realized she was right. "But we're going out tomorrow night, just for a little dinner. I think I'll eat with him, but make it very clear it's a one-time thing. As you said, Cracker, the Tylers are a big deal, and I don't want to offend him."

"Don't worry about offending him. Setting boundaries is important, and you can tell Cort no if you want to." Cracker said, then Therapista glanced at her watch and slid the puppet off her hand. "I'm sorry, Carter, but my next client will be here any minute. Are you feeling better?"

There was a pile of used tissues in my lap, so I grabbed them and stood up. Belinda pointed to the metal bin next to her desk and I tossed them inside. I was definitely confused, but felt a little calmer now. In a tiny voice, I replied to her question.

"Maybe?"

CHAPTER 12
ASHER

"What on earth were you thinking going to Carter's business?" Florida scolded me the minute I walked through Mom's back door. "Not once, but twice. Give the man a moment's peace, and he might like you again."

"How did you know I went twice?"

"Because it was my sister Georgia who told you to go away the first time. You've met her before. And I just got off the phone with Carter." She followed me from the tack room to the kitchen, bitching the entire time. "Poor Carter, how's he supposed to figure out what he wants when all you do is pester him? He's so sweet, handsome, and charming. Good lord, what a mess you've made, Asher."

I spun around and pointed my finger in her face. "Stop. Don't say another word about my relationship. If I wanted your opinion, I would've asked for it."

Florida grabbed my finger and bent it backward until I yelped. "If you'd listen to me in the first place, you wouldn't be in so much trouble."

"Damn it." I muttered, and scurried out of the kitchen, only to be faced with the ladies who drank. Oops, I meant lunched.

"Asher dear, you're just in time for tea." Granny smiled, and held up a crystal glass filled with a ruby red liquid that was definitely not tea. Mary Jane grinned, and Lila Brooke snored on the couch next to her. I was starving, and was grateful to see a three tier silver tray laden with finger sandwiches. There was no way in hell I was pressing Florida into cooking duty. She'd spit in my food, or worse.

I sat on the love seat opposite them, grabbed a salad plate, and loaded it with cucumber sandwiches and a couple of scones. "I need the hard stuff, not tea."

Granny nodded her head toward the bar, and I got up and fixed a vodka on the rocks. When I settled back on the sofa, Granny spoke. "Why are you home from work so early? Normally you don't arrive until dinner time, or later."

"Mom ordered me to patch things up with Carter, so she made me leave work." I said, then stuffed an entire cucumber sandwich in my mouth.

"How did that go, dear?" Mary Jane asked, then she discreetly elbowed Lila Brooke when she grunted in her sleep. Her partner's eyes snapped open, then she yawned and sat up straight.

"As well as can be expected when dealing with a high-strung drama queen whose thirst for theatrics knows no bounds." I grumbled and bit into an orange scone. "Florida is a pain in the ass, but God, the woman knows how to cook."

"I'm a pain in your ass because you're stupid." Florida entered the room, pushing a cart. She placed a clear glass teapot on the table next to the sandwiches. Why she did this, none of us knew, since we rarely, if ever, drank actual tea during tea.

"Thank you Florida." Granny smiled beatifically at her. "The food is tasty, as Asher just said."

"He also said I'm a pain in the ass." She rolled up a tea towel and threatened to snap me with it. I held up my arm, and she shook her head with disgust. "Use the head on your neck for once, and you can get your man back."

"Darling, what's the latest on Carter?" Lila Brooke asked.

"Nada. Zip. We're through." I felt numb. No more tears, just a dull ache that wouldn't go away. "Carter wants nothing to do with me. I went to see him this afternoon, and, I'm ashamed to say, we argued on the street in front of his shop."

All four women sucked in their breath.

"Did anyone we know see this?" Granny asked. "Because that's just plain..."

"Tacky." The other women muttered, shaking their heads.

"Nobody, if you don't count Karina and her customers. Oh, and the kids who wash hair." I crammed another cucumber sandwich in my mouth, and Florida smacked my shoulder.

"Stop eating like a degenerate. Your Mother didn't teach you bad manners."

"Oh dear." Mary Jane shook her head. "The entire country club will know about this by nightfall."

"What do you mean?" I asked, and Florida smacked me again.

"Don't talk with your mouth full."

I turned and glared at her, but she just put her hands on her bony hips and glared back. When I was a kid, Mom never hired a nanny, because Florida was my back-up mother. She drove me to school, took me to tennis lessons, and while all that was happening, she'd morphed into a cantankerous she-devil.

"Dearest Asher, you're so oblivious to the way our world works." Mary Jane frowned. "Karina does everyone who's anyone's hair, and her salon is gossip central. When your mother hears about this, she's going to..."

"When I hear about what, Mary Jane?" Mother strolled into the living room and went straight to the bar.

"You're home early, Mom." I said, and Florida took my plate and set it on the cart. "Hey, I wasn't finished eating!"

"You've had more than enough." Florida snapped. "Wasn't Carter upset you were outgrowing all your things? If you want Carter, you'd better get your figure back."

"Oh my God." I moaned into my hands.

"Well, Marjorie, it looks like Asher went to Carter's business, and they had a well, let's just say, a belligerent encounter on the street in front of Karina, and her customers." Mary Jane rolled her eyes.

"Asher," Mom sat next to me. "When I said you should fix this situation, I meant it. Personally, I don't care if you want to air your dirty laundry in the streets, but it could come back to haunt you."

"Mom, when I arrived at Carter's shop, another man was there with him."

Everyone gasped.

"What? Carter didn't tell me that..." Florida started, but I cut her off.

"Yes, there was another man there, and Mother," I turned to her. "It was Cort Tyler."

Mom's eyebrows drew together, then she sipped her drink and shut her eyes. "Please, please, please tell me nothing untoward was going on?"

"No, of course not. Sissy was there, and you know how she sticks her nose in everyone's business." I said, and like a Greek chorus, the ladies all mumbled, "Uh, huh."

"Indulge my curiosity, Asher." Mom sighed. "What was my employee doing at Carter's shop?"

Everyone drew in a deep breath. Cort was the one not thinking with the appropriate head.

"He asked Carter out on a date." My throat tightened, and I decided it was time for another drink. I stood and walked over to the bar. When I turned around, Mom was shaking her head with her bright pink lips pressed in a straight line. "As I told you already, I'd asked Cort to help me with Carter. Instead, he saw it as the perfect opportunity to make his move." I paused for dramatic effect. "Carter accepted his invitation."

"Cort is the most competitive man I've ever known," Mom muttered, and raised an eyebrow. "Which is why he's an excellent lawyer. But, he…"

"Fire his ass!" Florida interrupted.

"Yeah!" Lila Brooke and Mary Jane exclaimed.

"I can't do that." Mom blinked. "He'd sue me. But I will let him know that I'm not pleased. We've always had a good working relationship. Let's see if he values that relationship or not."

I felt fingers in my hair and glanced up to see Florida, who had a quizzical expression on her face.

"I love Carter, but this is the limit." She grumbled. "What's good for the goose is good for the gander. Do you know where they're going, honey?"

"No, but it's not too hard to find out." I could easily get Sissy to spill the beans. The woman couldn't keep a secret.

"Find yourself a man and show up where they're going to be." She kissed the top of my head. "Nobody messes with my family."

"So I'm in your good graces again?" I smiled up at her, and she clucked her tongue.

"Always were, except when you were doing stupid shit."

"Darling, if you want to do something like that, feel free. But I refuse to see our good name dragged through the mud." Mom went to the bar and started pouring another drink. "I can't decide for you, but I dare say that if Carter continues to act the way he is, it might be best to let him go." Mom said over her shoulder.

My chest tightened. I'd do anything to win Carter back, but Mom had a point. So far, I'd been reduced to arguing with him on the street. What was next? Fist fights? Not only would that accomplish nothing, it could hurt my family's reputation, and the business.

"Fine, I'll give it one last shot. If it doesn't work, I'll…"

Mary Jane slid a plate of brownies across the table and nodded her head. "Go on, eat one. It'll make you feel better."

I rarely ate her special brownies, but today was hellish. After biting into one, I realized that one important aspect of this plan might be difficult to work out.

"Where the hell am I going to find a man to go on a date with?"

CHAPTER 13

ASHER

"Just go to a bar and pick someone up." Mary Jane said, but there was no way I could do that. "You're a catch. Men would pay to go out with you."

"Yeah, but I don't like the idea of leading some guy on. It needs to be with someone who knows this is only a fake date." I sighed. "Oh, and Carter can't know the guy either. Otherwise he'll find out it's not real."

"Back in our day, men kept little black books with names and phone numbers of all the people they were interested in. So much easier than nowadays, what with all the online dating apps." Lila Brooke shook her head. "I don't understand how people even meet each other anymore."

"Be right back." I got to my feet and went into the library. I needed to discover where Carter was going on his date before I even bothered to find someone to go out with me. My fingers trembled as I placed the call to my former mother-in-law.

"Asher, darling." Sissy answered on the first ring. "I'm in my car, so it's safe to talk."

"Oh Sissy, this has become one giant disaster." I grumbled. "Can you help me to…"

"Anything you want, just ask. Carter is being stupid. In fact, I don't think he even likes that man. He's just being a drama queen." I heard a car horn beep through the phone. "Oops, sorry. Oh, not you, Asher. I didn't see the light turn green."

"Would it be better if I called you at home later?"

"No, this is the safest place, because Carter's not with me. You never know when he's going to turn up at the house." Sissy sighed. "I will do anything to bring you boys back together. Carter even mentioned a new wedding at the country club a few days ago. It's like he's totally lost his mind. That's exactly what he wants, yet he's throwing it all away."

"Thank you, Sissy." Maybe I'd underestimated my mother-in-law over the years. She apparently had my back. "What I need to know is where Carter and Cort are going on their date."

"Why do you need to know that?" Another car horn blared through the phone. "Asher, give me a second. I'm going to pull into this parking lot here so I can pay better attention."

"Sure." Given how flighty Sissy could be, that was understandable. A few moments later, she returned to the phone call.

"There. I needed to go to Whole Foods anyway, and here I am. So, why do you want to know where Carter and that man are going?" She asked, and I heard her get out of the car.

"If I tell you, promise me you won't say a word to Carter."

"Oh dear." Sissy sighed, then said 'thanks' to somebody. "Have you ever thought that the two of you need to stop playing games and just be honest with each other?"

"I've tried that, which ended up with us on the street making fools of ourselves." My head started humming, and I realized it was the brownie I'd eaten a few minutes ago. "Promise me you won't say anything to Carter, and I'll tell you."

"Fine." Sissy huffed. "Excuse me, I want a pint of the organic crab dip. Thanks."

"This is the last attempt to make things right with Carter. If this doesn't work, we're through."

"I can't blame you one bit, Asher." Sissy said. "I love my son, but he's a handful on the best of days."

"If you tell me where Carter and Cort are going on their date, I'm going to show up with a date of my own." I resisted the urge to giggle. Damn brownie. "You know, what's good for the goose is good for the gander."

"They're going to L'Opossum, that quirky restaurant in Oregon Hill. I've never been there myself, but I hear it's fabulous." Sissy whispered. Why, I didn't know since she was in the middle of a grocery store.

"Thanks, Sissy."

————

Since I didn't know where to find a date, Mom suggested going to a gay bar. So, I ordered an Uber and headed downtown.

Carter and I met the old fashioned way, in person at a friend's wedding. He'd been the best man at Carrie and Mike Florman's marriage, and from the moment I set eyes on him I knew Carter was the man for me. We'd never hung out at gay bars, and I rarely went to them before I met him. Now I was in the backseat of an old man's Honda heading to Barcode, a place I'd only been to a handful of times. Granny, Lila Brooke and Mary Jane had wanted to tag along, but I knew they'd frighten off any potential dates.

"We're here, sir." The older man turned in his seat and winked. "Hope you get lucky."

"Uh, thanks." I let myself out and stood on the sidewalk, willing myself to go inside. The reason I'd never been into the bar scene, or dating apps, was how impersonal they were. That didn't mean I hadn't had my share of one-night-stands, but they were usually with people I had some sort of connection with. Standing in a bar, forcing myself to talk to people I didn't know wasn't my idea of fun.

"Asher Yates?"

I turned at the sound of my name and saw a guy I'd gone to school with, Ted Berling. At UVA we'd shared a love of horseback riding, which turned into a passion for fox hunting. Once we graduated, he'd gone on to medical school while I'd studied law.

"Ted, good to see you, man." We did a brief bro hug, then Ted held open the door to the bar, and I strolled inside. "I'm glad you're here. It's been ages since I was in a gay bar."

"It's still the same. Men looking for love in all the wrong places." Ted slapped my back, and we went up to the bar to place our orders. "Hey, I heard through the grapevine that you're married now."

"Uh, yeah. Well, it's complicated." I replied, then ordered a vodka on the rocks from a drag queen with violet hair and enormous boobs. Once our drinks were in front of us, Ted led me to a table.

"All relationships are complicated." Ted grinned. "That's why I'm relentlessly single. Don't need the drama or the hassle of a boyfriend."

"When did we see each other last?"

"Oh, it must have been almost ten years ago at graduation." Ted sipped his drink. "You don't get out much, do you?"

"No." I muttered, then studied my old friend's face. Ted was attractive enough, though he was one of the biggest snobs I'd ever met. "Have you ever met Carter Camden?"

"No, never heard of him." Ted said. "Why?"

Ted was from a prominent family, and from what I remembered, he came from money, too. Just the man to make Carter jealous. I wondered if he would be the perfect so-called date? "Ted, I have a proposition for you, and if you say yes, I'll be forever grateful."

"Sure. What is it?"

———

"So you want me to be your fake date?" Ted laughed. "I'm the most anti-relationship guy you'll ever meet, but for you? The man who got me into the most exclusive fraternity at UVA? Sure. Glad to help."

"Oh God, thank you Ted." For the first time in days, I felt a tiny sliver of hope. "You don't know how much this means to me."

Ted picked up his drink and eyed me. "So, what I want to know is why? From everything you've told me, Carter is a lot of drama. Like, does he have the dick of death or something?"

I drummed my fingers on the table while I tried to find the right words. "He's the only person I've ever met who makes me happy. When we're not arguing, that is. Carter is very attractive, witty, and well, he's also amazing in the sack, though it's been awhile. With him, it's not just sex, it's making love. He's everything I've ever wanted in a husband. Oh, and you've met my family, right?"

"The eccentric Yates clan? They're a legend. I remember them driving up to Charlottesville in a Bentley, which made all our fraternity brothers jealous as hell. They were there for a fox hunt, if I remember right. But what really stands out in my mind is when your grandmother and her friends showed up at the fraternity party that night and drank all our alcoholic brothers under the table." Ted laughed.

"Well, Carter fits in with my family like nobody else could.

And you're right, they are a bunch of lunatics." I finished the drink and grabbed my phone to summon an Uber. "Thanks for doing this. Just meet me at L'Opossum tomorrow night at seven." I stood up, and Ted grabbed my arm.

"Hey, so how affectionate should I act toward you? I don't want to piss this guy off, but hey, this is my first and probably only chance to go on a date with you." Ted winked, and I remembered how he'd once come on to me when we were in school. He did nothing for me then, and the same could be said for today.

"Just follow my lead. Whatever Carter and Cort do, we'll do the exact same thing."

CHAPTER 14

CARTER

"I'm surprised you can breathe. I've never seen so much dust." Georgia bitched from the dining room. I liked Florida's sister. She was slower, but very thorough. Plus, she was handy with a needle and thread, and had hemmed a pair of slacks I'd bought for tonight's date with Cort. They were black velvet cords with a white waistband. I was wearing them with a crimson t-shirt and a matching black velvet jacket. Shiny, black Ferragamo loafers completed the look.

I grabbed a tube of concealer off the bathroom counter, then patted some of it under my eyes, and on a tiny zit next to my left eyebrow. Whenever I had problems sleeping, I woke up the next day with the dark circles of a raccoon, and the zits of a fifteen-year-old. Normally I slept eight hours a night, like a normal person. Now that I was single again, I was lucky to get five hours, and that was with the help of sleeping pills.

"Carter, I need a brush from under the sink." I jumped at Georgia's voice. She was standing in the doorway, so I moved aside so she could get what she wanted. "Oh, hand me that lint brush." She pointed to it on the counter. "You've got dust bunnies on your back."

I held my arms out, and she brushed the dust off. "You nervous about your big date, sweetie?"

"A little," I sighed. "I'm only going out with him the one time. He's from a big-deal family, so it would look bad if I turned him down." There was nothing I'd like to do more than call Cort up and cancel. I'd tossed and turned all night, because although Asher and I weren't married, it felt like I was cheating on him. It was ridiculous, but I knew I wasn't ready to date Cort, or anyone else, for that matter. Before I accepted another date from someone, I had to get over Asher first. It wasn't fair to me, or the date if I was still in love with my former husband.

"You still got it bad for Asher?" Georgia spun me around and brushed the front of my jacket.

"Yeah. But I have to get over him, since he never wanted to be married in the first place."

"Florida and I talked on the phone last night." Georgia placed the brush on the bathroom counter and crossed her arms over her ample chest. "We think you're blowing everything out of proportion."

Why the hell were they talking about me behind my back? I must have made a face because she backed out of the bathroom into the hallway.

"So, what brought you to that conclusion?" I grabbed the styling gel out of the medicine cabinet and began fixing my hair.

"Never mind." Georgia spun around to leave.

"Wait."

She didn't turn around, so I addressed her back. "Please enlighten me. Why do you and your sister think I'm over-reacting?"

Her shoulders slumped. "Well, what happened was a

mistake, and Asher was trying to make things better by getting married again." She turned around and held her hands out like she was praying. "That man is miserable without you, and from what I can see, you ain't much better."

My eyes shut, and all I could see was Asher's face. "I miss him. Hell, I miss all the Yates family." I felt Georgia's hands smoothing out the front of my jacket, so I opened my eyes to behold the warmest smile on her face.

"There's an easy way to make things better, Carter." She inhaled. "Forgive him and make things right between the two of you. You're both crazy about each other. Asher didn't mean what he said about not wanting to be married. According to Florida, you two had a fight the night before, and you kicked him out of the bedroom. So the next day, you ask him if he still wanted to be married, or if he had to do it all over again. Shit, I can't keep this mess straight in my head. Anyhow, can you blame him for saying, 'No, I wish I wasn't married to you'?"

She had a point. My sinuses burned, the first signal that waterworks were on the way. "I can't cry right now. My date will be here any minute, and even though this is the only date we'll go on, I can't open the front door blubbering about Asher to his friend. Hell, I doubt they're friends anymore after tonight." I grabbed a few tissues and put them in the inner pocket of my jacket. The way I was feeling, I'd probably need them at some point tonight.

The doorbell rang, and I froze.

"Want me to get that?" Georgia patted my shoulder, and I dabbed at my eyes with a tissue.

"Yes, please."

———

"What a charming little restaurant." I forced a smile on my face as a hostess seated us in a booth toward the rear of the dark dining room. A French disco song was playing in the background, and whatever was cooking in the kitchen smelled amazing. "I'm shocked Asher and, oh, sorry. Shouldn't mention him, I guess."

Cort grinned. "The elephant in the room has already made his presence known." He reached across the table and patted my hand. "It's okay to talk about Asher. I mean, he was your husband."

"Sort of." I mumbled, though in my heart he always had been my husband. Even the drama of our former relationship couldn't erase my feelings for Asher. "Okay. Well, Asher and I never came here. You know, to this restaurant. What neighborhood is this again?"

"Oregon Hill. I own a couple of apartment buildings on Laurel Street. Being a lawyer is my job, but renovating old buildings is my passion." Cort picked up the menu. "Do you like Zinfandel?"

I nodded.

"The Tom of Finland Zinfandel is wonderful. Let's order a bottle when the waitress returns." Cort said, and for the first time in my life, I struggled to think of something to talk about. I was so used to being with Asher that I didn't know what to say to this man.

"So, um, you're into real estate?"

"Yeah, it's in the blood. I grew up on the family plantation, Sherwood Forest." Cort pulled his phone out, tapped on the screen, then handed it to me.

"Oh, wow. This is a stunning home." I handed him the phone back. Normally, I would love to talk about houses and design. It's what I did for a living, but I felt empty. "I bet it takes a lot of upkeep."

"It's been in the family since my great-great-great-grandfather, President Tyler, bought it in 1842." Cort drawled, and I was unimpressed with his obvious bragging. "It's constantly being renovated, otherwise it would've fallen apart decades ago. My Dad taught me everything there is to know about the care and upkeep of older homes. When a few properties went up for sale in Oregon Hill, I snapped them up. Now a real estate management firm rents them out for me. My goal is to have a real estate empire so I can retire from practicing law."

"You don't enjoy working for..."

"Gentlemen, my name is Elisa, and I'm your server tonight." A woman with red hair the same color as Cort's interrupted. "What can I get you to drink?"

Cort ordered the bottle of wine, and I was curious about what he'd said earlier. "So, you don't enjoy being a lawyer?"

"Well, it's okay. But let me tell you a little secret." He leaned over the table and whispered, "I hate working for Marjorie."

"What?" I was genuinely confused. She was like a second mother to me.

"When her husband passed away, she took full control of the business." Cort began, but the server dropped the bottle of wine off. After filling our glasses, I urged him to continue. "He was a great guy, easy going, and relaxed. Well, relaxed for a lawyer, that is. Then Marjorie took over, and everything changed."

"Wasn't she the firm's biggest producer even before he died?" I'd swear that's what Asher told me.

"Oh yes. Despite her being half-drunk most of the time, she's a shark." Cort sipped the wine and sighed. "The problem is, she's a woman."

"You've got to be kidding me." I shook my head in disgust. Why did I agree to go out with this man again?

"Now it's all work. We used to have fun, but when he died,

Marjorie was hell-bent on making it the number one firm in the state. And she did, but that's not what I signed up for." Cort shook his head. "Though I'm the best lawyer at the firm, it's not what I love. In fact, I'm thinking of getting my real estate license and quitting."

Ah. So that's why Cort didn't mind pissing off the Yates family. He was planning on leaving. "From what I've been told, you're fantastic at what you do." I honestly didn't know what else to say. God, blowhards bored me.

"As I said, I'm the... oh my God." Cort's eyes widened. "I can't believe he's here."

"Who?" I swiveled my head around, then froze. "Why is that ugly man holding Asher's hand?"

CHAPTER 15

ASHER

Cort's mouth dropped open when we entered the restaurant. I winked at him. He turned scarlet, then Carter turned in their booth to get a look. His mouth opened, shut, then he turned back to Cort.

"Gentlemen." The hostess seated us across the dining room from Carter and Cort. It was close enough to see them, but far enough away I couldn't hear what they were saying. Every few seconds, Carter would glance over at me and Ted. Cort took his hand, and to my delight, Carter snatched it away.

"I know him." Ted whispered. "Isn't that Cort Tyler?"

"Yes." I grinned. "He works at mother's law firm. Well, for now, that is. If I had to bet money on it, I'd say he won't be with us much longer."

"Your husband is hot." Ted winked. "Oops, sorry. Your not husband is hot."

"Yes, he is. Thankfully, he doesn't think so." I opened the menu. "One of the best things about Carter is his lack of vanity. He dresses well, takes care of himself, but it's all because he feels unattractive. Doesn't matter how many times I tell him he's the best looking man in the world, he never believes me."

I glanced over to Carter's booth and realized I didn't have a clear view of him thanks to a table in the center aisle blocking my view. That's when I noticed a mirror on the wall right behind them. Looking there, I could see both their faces at the same time.

"Gentlemen, my name is Elisa and I'll be your server this evening." She had red hair the same color as Cort's, and a tiny diamond stud in her nose. "What can I get you to drink?"

"Vodka on the rocks, top shelf." I replied, and Ted ordered a Scotch. Once the waitress was gone, we resumed spying on Carter and Cort. Apparently, Carter couldn't see me peeking at them through the mirror, and every thirty seconds he'd crane his head to stare at us. Honestly, I was admiring his restraint. He crossed his arms over his chest, and his lower lip stuck out like a pissed-off teenager.

"Okay, so what's next?" Ted whispered. "Do you want me to act frisky with you?"

"No, not yet. Let's allow the moment to build." I replied, and an odd feeling of satisfaction spread through my limbs. Cort's face matched his hair color, while Carter was frantically whispering something. He attempted a smile, but instead, Carter bared his clenched teeth. He had been giving me hell for days now, and it felt good watching him react to me and Ted's presence. "Okay, let's turn up the heat a little."

The waitress dropped off our drinks, and as soon as she was gone, I reached across the booth and took his hand, keeping my eyes on the mirror behind Carter.

"Well now, I never knew you cared." Ted giggled. "Ooh! Look at him!"

Carter's fists clenched, and I knew it was taking every ounce of self-control he had, which wasn't much, to keep from flying off the handle. One of his arms twitched, and his wine glass fell to the floor with a crash.

"Goddamnit!" He yelled, then his back straightened. Cort snuck a glance at us, and at that moment I knew how miserable he must be feeling. Served the bastard right. The waitress rushed over with a fresh glass and began cleaning up the mess. I could tell from Carter's pinched expression that he desperately wanted to say something. But, he couldn't until the server left. A moment later, he was whispering to Cort. Then, Carter took Cort's hand and attempted to gaze at him adoringly. It was fake, I could tell. But, now that Carter was upping the ante, I escalated things.

"Ted." I leaned over the table and whispered, "come sit next to me on this side of the booth."

"Are you sure?" Ted's eyes darkened. I knew why. In our social circles, public displays of affection were frowned upon. Holding my hand was one thing, but such close proximity was rarely done.

"Yes, I'm positive." I patted the seat next to me, and Ted rose to his feet and sat.

"Direct hit." Ted whispered, nodding toward them. Carter's mouth hung open, and Cort had his face in his hands. Damned asshole knew when he was beaten. Carter stomped over to our table.

"Whoever you are, stop it right now." Carter fumed, pointing at Ted. "I know this isn't an actual date you're on, Asher. You're doing it to hurt me."

I put my arm over Ted's shoulders and smiled. "Carter, you're the one who said you had to get on with your life. Well," I pecked Ted's cheek, "I'm getting on with my life."

Carter's lips twisted, then Cort was by his side. Instead of a red face, he now looked green. He put his arm around Carter's waist, and Carter stepped away from Cort and hissed, "Don't touch me!"

I waggled my fingers at Cort, who sighed, then walked right out the door.

"Are you satisfied, Asher? Do you feel like more of a man now that you've ruined my date?" He pressed his lips together, and I could see the beginning of a vertical line forming between his eyebrows. I wanted to kiss him right there.

"I think you did that yourself, Carter." I removed my arm from Ted's shoulders and smiled. "You just told Cort to take his hands off you. What's a guy to think? So he left. No loss. You can do much better than that snobby prick."

"I um, well." Carter shook his head dramatically, then sat across from Ted and me. Then he pointed at Ted. "Are you guys on an actual date?"

"No." Ted rose to his feet. "I'm leaving now." Ted patted my shoulder. "Asher, I guess I'll see you again in a few years or so." Then he strolled out of the restaurant.

"Sir, did you want to eat at this table?" The waitress asked Carter, who tilted his head in my direction.

"Yes, he does." I replied, and the server brought a barely touched bottle of red wine and Carter's glass to him. "Would you like to hear today's specials? We have a lovely…"

"No." Carter and I said at the same time. The woman shrugged her shoulders and took off. We stared at each other, neither saying a word for what seemed a very long time. Finally, Carter drained his glass of wine and spoke.

"What do we have to do to make things better? Because I love you, and if that ugly fake date was any indication, you love me too."

———

We didn't bother ordering food. Instead, we killed the bottle of wine and ordered another. I didn't drive here, and neither did Carter, so we didn't worry about drinking too much. Plus, we needed something to loosen us up. Talking was hard when you wanted to take the love of your life in your arms and kiss all the problems away.

The thing was, I knew if we went back to our old relationship and didn't put effort into our marriage, we'd repeat the same mistakes. What I was about to propose to Carter would probably shock him.

"Asher, you're the love of my life." He laid his hand on mine, and it felt so damned right. But I forced myself to move my hand away. "Hey, you don't believe me?"

I stared into his sensual dark eyes, wondering how I was going to put this into words. "I believe you. And I feel the same for you, Carter. I've never loved anyone like you before, and I promise you I'll love no one else. But..."

"But what?" Carter leaned back, and I loved how the candlelight warmed up his black blazer.

"Things have to change."

"Well, obviously." Carter sniffed, then topped up his glass. He swirled the red liquid around, then set it back on the table. "I want our new wedding to be planned by Lori Stallings. She's the best, and I promise you it will be... why are you shaking your head like that?"

"I'm not marrying you unless a few things change first." I sighed. Nothing would please me more than to walk down the aisle with Carter, but unless certain conditions were met, I refused. "I refuse to be kicked out of our bedroom again, and I refuse to engage in juvenile theatrics whenever you don't get your way. Carter, I hate to tell you this, but you're spoiled rotten."

"What! Me?" Carter winked. He knew I spoke the truth.

"Okay, I'll admit that I can be a little temperamental. But marriage is a two-way street, and there are things you need to work on too. So tell me, what do I have to change to make our relationship work?"

I leaned back and grinned into the wine glass. "If you hadn't heard, I love you more than life itself. I don't want you to change who you are, but there is one thing I need in order to move forward."

"Anything Asher." Carter swiped at his eyes and laid his hand on mine again. This time, I turned my palm over and squeezed.

"I want you to woo me."

CHAPTER 16

CARTER

"Pardon me?"

"You heard me, Carter. I want to be courted, made love to. Hell, you can even seduce me." Asher squeezed my hand. "I want a new beginning for us. And honestly, I feel like when we first met, I did most of the courting. Now it's my turn to be wooed."

My stomach flipped, remembering the early days of our romance. Asher would take me to dinners, parties, and plays. He'd flown me to New York for spur-of-the-moment trips, and was constantly bringing me little gifts. The thought of making him feel the way I did when he lavished me with romantic surprises made my pulse ramp up.

"Asher, you are the owner of my heart. If you want to be properly courted, I'm happy to oblige." I murmured, then kissed his hand. He still had his wedding ring on, while I'd taken mine off before going out with that bore, Cort. God, this man really loved me. "What would you like me to do first? Buy you flowers? Or how about we spend a long weekend in the Bahamas? Karina told me about…"

"Don't tell me." Asher grinned. "Surprise me, Carter."

"I hate to admit this, but I'm unsure of how to impress you."
I said and meant it. "You grew up with enormous wealth, and
because of that, you've done just about anything in the world
you wanted. It's like buying a gift for a gazillionaire who
already has everything they could ever want."

Asher blushed. He always did when I mentioned money.
"I'm not asking for expensive gifts, or trips. What I want is to
feel valued and loved. Hell, you could give me a handwritten
love letter and that would mean more to me than any material
possessions you could buy."

"Oh." I sighed. "Do you feel like I don't love you, because if
that's the case, you're so wrong. I value you and our relationship more than anything else in the world."

"If that's the case, why did you abandon me so easily?"
Asher let go of my hand, and blood raced up my neck. How
dare he think I was at fault for the sad state of our marriage.
Cracker's advice came to me, so I closed my eyes and began
taking deep breaths. "What are you doing?"

Calm washed through me, so I opened my eyes and smiled.
"Calming myself. First, it took a lot to get me upset enough to
leave you. Second, our original marriage not being real was
neither of our faults." God, I couldn't believe I saw it so clearly
now. "I overreacted without thinking everything through, and
for that, I'm sorry."

"I'm sorry too." Asher murmured. "Mom told me not to tell
you about the marriage fiasco, and like an idiot, I obeyed her."

"Marjorie?" My eyebrows shot up, and Asher nodded. Then
I realized Asher wasn't the only one who'd taken terrible
advice. "My mother told me the same thing." I scratched my
chin. "Why didn't they want us to work through this problem
with honesty?"

"We are talking about our mothers." Asher chuckled. "Mom

always views problems through the lens of the law. She said that my assets were better protected if I didn't tell you our marriage wasn't legal."

"Really?" My eyes rolled. "I'm kind of disappointed in her. But then, my mother wasn't any better. She didn't want me to lose the money and status of being a Yates. Mom is such a snob."

"I'm not surprised." Asher stated. "Our families are insane. All they think about is money." Asher's face darkened. "You didn't marry me for my..."

"No, oh God, no." I picked up his hand and brought it to my lips. "I would've fallen in love with you regardless of your wealth. Or perhaps, maybe not?"

Asher's face lost all color.

"Wait, don't get upset. Let me explain." I kissed his hand, and he snatched it away. "Asher, you wouldn't be the man you are if you hadn't grown up a Yates, with all the prestige and money. Life experiences mold us, shape us into the men we are. For example, if you hadn't been rich, you probably wouldn't have gone to UVA and become one of the best lawyers in the state. Face it, sweetie. If you'd been born into a poor family, you might still have become a lawyer, but do you truly believe you'd be a full partner in the state's biggest law firm at thirty-two? Without the privilege you were born with, you would have a very different life."

Asher's shoulders relaxed. "I guess you've got a point. So would you have loved me if I'd been a construction worker, or a cop? I could have been a firefighter, or..."

"Darling, if you say an Indian or a cowboy next, I'll know you secretly want to be a member of the Village People." I bit my lip to keep from laughing at my silly joke.

"And that's one of the reasons I love you so much. The wittiest man alive, and the sexiest." Asher stood up, then sat next to me on my side of the booth. "With all my heart, I love you, Carter. Maybe we shouldn't listen to our families so much."

"Most of them are certifiable." I murmured, unable to take my eyes off of him.

"What's that old statistic?" Asher put his arm over my shoulders. "I think it's one out of every four people has a mental illness. Take a close look at your friends and family, and if they're all normal, look in the mirror."

"Honey, everyone we know is loony." I giggled, "Including us."

"Gentlemen, the kitchen is about to close. Would you care for anything else?" The server asked, breaking the cozy spell that had fallen over us. We were the only people left in the restaurant.

"No, thank you." I replied. "Check please."

———

"I don't want the night to end just yet." Asher said when we left L'Opossum. "The river's only a couple of blocks from here. I want to see it with you in the moonlight."

I held my hand out, and he took it. "You can see the river from our backyard, but if you insist." I grinned, and we strolled down China Street. "The moon is full, and there's not a cloud in the sky."

"It's gorgeous." Asher remarked, and it was. Neither of us said a word until we came along a little park overlooking the river. There was a tiny yellow gazebo in the center, and I led us to it. "I love the reflection of the moon on the water."

"Me too." Asher put his arm around my waist and I melted into him. His woodsy scent filled my nose, and I turned and held him in my arms. "I've missed this, Carter.

Just holding you makes all of my problems seem a million miles away."

"I don't want to fight anymore." My voice sounded thick, and a tear slid down the side of my nose. Asher gripped me tight against him, then he lifted my face with his finger under my chin. He swiped my tears away with his thumb. "It's been awful. I can't sleep or concentrate on anything. We can't let this ever happen again."

"No baby, we can't." Asher kissed my forehead, then my cheeks. "I need to kiss you, Carter."

"You never have to ask." I swallowed, then tilted my head up. "Please, kiss me like you mean it, Asher."

His lips hovered over mine for a long moment, and Asher's blue eyes twinkled.

"Please, what are you waiting for?"

Asher's lips brushed over mine, and I trembled in his arms, then he tightened his grip on me, and his warm, wet lips crashed into mine. I groaned, and my knees felt weak. Asher's tongue dipped into my mouth, and our noses bumped into each other's. I loved the scrape of his five-o'clock shadow on the skin around my lips. His warm hands spread across the back of my neck, then his fingers gripped my hair and the kiss deepened further. Asher was the love of my life, an undeniable fact made even more real by the way my heart pounded in my chest. Nothing or no one had ever made me feel so passionate, so loved.

Asher's hard cock pressed against my lower stomach, and the urge to drop to my knees and take him in my mouth filled me. Then a bright light shone on us. We jumped apart, both of us panting with desire.

"Gentlemen." The flashlight was blinding, especially since we couldn't see who was holding it. Then the light pointed down, and I blinked. "I'm Officer Smith. It's wonderful that you're enjoying the beautiful view of the river, but perhaps you need to take this inside."

My heart was pounding so hard from both Asher and the cop. "Of course, sir." I mumbled, then Asher took my hand, and we started walking back into the Oregon Hill neighborhood. The feel of his smooth palm against mine was nearly as good as our kiss. All I wanted now was to wake up in his arms in the morning, and have everything go back to the way it used to be. When we got back to the restaurant, all the windows were dark. Asher fished his phone out of his pocket and started tapping on the screen. I figured he was calling a car, so I leaned against the building, a lone streetlight shining down on the two of us.

"How far away is the driver?" I asked.

"It's only two blocks away." Asher grinned, then pecked me on the cheek. "Aren't you going to call a car, too?"

"Huh? Call a car?" Why the hell would we take two cars?

CHAPTER 17
ASHER

"Carter, we don't live together anymore. We can share a ride if you like, but I meant what I said." I loved this man so much, but things had to change first. "I want to be courted, and I want us to work on our issues before we get remarried."

Carter bit his lower lip, then did the strange breathing thing with his eyes closed again. After a few seconds, he opened them and grinned. "You're right, Asher. I guess I was expecting things to automatically return to the way they used to be."

I laid my hands on his shoulders and locked my eyes with his. "Remember, the reason we broke up in the first place was miscommunication, and keeping secrets from each other. Let's do better this time, then we can have the wedding of your dreams."

Carter's gaze dropped, and a slow smile spread across his cheeks. "Okay. Can we agree on one thing first?"

I nodded, wondering what he wanted.

"When we originally got married, we did it your way, in private, on top of that mountain. I want our next ceremony done my way." He said, then the car pulled up. "May I share the ride with you?"

"Yes, of course." I slid open the back door of a lime-green minivan and Carter climbed in first. After telling the driver where Carter's shop was, we sat back in the seat. I placed my hand on his, then Carter's fingers laced through mine.

"I want a big ceremony, so I can show the world how much I love you." Carter whispered, and the driver turned up the radio. It was the perfect music to end the night, Chopin's Nocturne in E-flat Major. Carter hated classical music, said it put him to sleep. I loved the piano and took lessons as a child. "I want the ceremony held at the country club, and I want the most important people in our lives to be there. Do you think I could get Florida in the ceremony somehow? Like an attendant of some sort? Because she means the world to me, and…"

"Anything for you, Carter. In fact, go ahead and start planning it." I squeezed his hand, and his face split in a smile. "But before we make things final, I want us to work through our problems." I leaned over and kissed his cheek. "And I wasn't kidding about being wooed."

"Hey, would you mind if I scheduled an appointment for the two of us with Belinda Therapista? You know, like marriage counseling?" Carter tilted his head while I struggled to find a reason not to say no. Dr. Johnson was nice, but I hated the thought of telling an almost stranger what was going on in my head. "Asher, you said we needed to work through our problems, and that's what a psychologist does."

I forced a smile onto my face. "You're right. Set up an appointment."

"Goody." Carter grinned, then the driver turned onto Cary Street a block from Carter's shop. "Sir, just pull into that parking lot."

It took all my self-control not to invite him back to the

house, but I wanted the time and space for us to work through our problems. Jumping back into our relationship too soon might end up killing it. "Good night, sweetheart. I love you."

Carter brushed his lips across mine and opened the minivan door. "I love you too, Asher Yates. Never forget that."

The door shut, and the driver backed out of the parking lot. I turned in the seat to watch Carter go up the back stairs. A streetlight in the alley was over him, and Carter's wavy black hair glistened. He leaned against the railing, brought his palm to his lips, then blew a kiss in my direction. I did the same, then the car turned onto Cary street, and began the long drive home.

————

When the driver turned onto the driveway, there was only one light shining in the house. It was my mother's study, and instead of having the driver drop me off at the cottage, I got out at the back door.

"Thanks." I muttered, then let myself into the tack room.

"Is that you, Asher?" Florida's sleepy voice called out. She had a small apartment on the first floor attached to the kitchen, and I must have woken her up.

"Yes." I whispered. "Go back to sleep."

I tiptoed through the dark first floor, then crept up the stairs. As usual with old homes, the hard wood creaked with every other step. When I got to the third floor, the door to Mom's study was open.

"Knock knock." I softly announced myself. Mom was behind the desk where she was doing paperwork.

"Darling." She murmured, gesturing for me to sit in the leather wingback chair in front of the desk. I shut the door, then sat down. "This has been quite an interesting evening. So, according to Cort, you and Carter have reconciled. Where is he?"

I rubbed my chin, confused. "Uh, Carter is sleeping in his loft over the shop. So enlighten me about something. Why did Cort tell you that?"

"Cort Tyler thought it best to call me, and he put in his notice." Mom sighed. "He's an excellent lawyer, and part of me wanted to refuse him. But, if he's going to be disloyal to our family, it's best that he leave. There are numerous ways he could sabotage the firm, so instead of trying to stop him, I thanked him for his work over the years and hung up. He'll be gone in two weeks." Mom shrugged her shoulders. "I know the two of you were close, but..."

"Mom, we weren't that close. He was someone I played tennis with, that's all." I sighed with relief. "I'm kind of shocked that Cort did the respectable thing."

"The Tylers are an old family, and despite Cort's betrayal, he knows the proper thing to do." Mom lifted a tumbler of what I presumed was vodka to her lips. "If he hadn't resigned, it would've forced my hand. Since we can no longer trust the man, I would've found a way to make him leave."

I'd seen Mom in action before, and she was ruthless. The last associate to piss her off went from litigating high-profile cases to representing clients in traffic court. He was gone in a matter of weeks.

"So, darling, why did Carter choose to sleep above his shop?"

"Actually, I wanted him to." I rubbed my temples with my fingers. "We can't ever go back to our old relationship. I made it clear to Carter that we have to make things better before getting married again. So, I've agreed to go to couples counseling with him."

Mom's eyebrow shot up.

"But I've told him to start planning the perfect wedding. Well, the perfect wedding for him and the family. If I had my way, we'd go to a justice of the peace. Instead, he wants to hold the ceremony at the country club. If that makes him happy, I'm all for it."

"Well, it sounds like you two have made progress." Mom said while gathering the paperwork in front of her and placing it in a folder. "And Mom will be happy. She loves big events, while I'm more like you. Your father and I had an enormous wedding at Sacred Heart Cathedral, and I hated all the fuss. Your first marriage to Carter was ideal in my opinion, but don't tell him I said that. Let him believe that you and I are thrilled by an elaborate ceremony. It will keep any drama to a minimum."

My gaze met Mom's, and we both giggled. "Carter is like the Peanuts character, Pigpen. But instead of dirt following in his wake, it's over-the-top drama."

"Oh, darling, I know." She shook her head. "That's why he fits in so well with the rest of our family. You and I are the sane lawyers, while they're…"

"Mom, drama…"

"Are you sure you want to marry him again? Because Carter made you insane, what with all his theatrics. While I always found it amusing, I could tell it wore on your nerves." Mom rose from her seat and switched off the desk lamp, my cue that this conversation was wrapping up.

"Mom, the marriage isn't that important to me, but Carter is. Hell, why do you think I agreed to visit Belinda Therapista with him?" I got to my feet and followed Mom into the hallway. "I've only met her a few times at the club. While she's certainly very attractive, she seemed kind of flighty to me. Plus, I only feel comfortable airing my dirty laundry in front of family."

Mom shut the door and yawned. "Sweetheart, if you feel in

your heart that marrying Carter is the right thing for you, then, by all means, do it. But life is short, and poor decisions can lead to a lifetime filled with regret." Mom placed her hands on my shoulders. "Now indulge me with a little bit of honesty. Do you love Carter enough to marry him all over again? Even knowing how tempestuous your relationship can be?

I shut my eyes for a moment and sighed. "Yes. I love him, Mom, more than anything else in the world. If a marriage will make him happy, then we'll have the biggest wedding Richmond's ever seen."

Mom pecked my cheek, then strolled down the hallway to her suite of rooms. When she got to her door, she turned around and smiled. "Carter will once again become a Yates, and you, my precious boy, will marry the love of your life. I wish you much luck and happiness. Goodnight."

The door shut behind her, and I strolled to the stairs. When I got to the landing, I paused for a moment. "Is getting married again a good thing, or am I setting myself up for more chaos?"

CHAPTER 18
CARTER

"Oh yes, Asher." I mumbled, then my eyes fluttered open, and I realized I was humping the mattress with my morning wood. "Jesus, that was one hell of a dream." I turned onto my back, then squeezed my erection. Asher was the only man in the world who could turn me on with just a glance of his sapphire-blue eyes. This would be the perfect morning for a little tumble in the sheets before heading to work, but unfortunately for me, I was in this bed alone.

Compared to most people I knew, I was a late bloomer. I didn't lose my virginity until I was twenty-two, and could count the number of men I'd slept with on one hand. It wasn't because of a lack of interest in sex. I'd been busy getting my degree, and unlike most of the people I knew, sex was only enjoyable with a man I had feelings for.

Belinda Therapista told me there was nothing wrong with me, that I was a demisexual. At the time, I'd thought, damn, I'm both a homosexual, and a demisexual. How many more categories would I be slotted into? Personally, I hated being labeled, but apparently most people needed labels to help understand themselves better. For me, it was unnecessary. I was Carter Camden-Yates. Oh yeah, just Carter Camden, but not for long.

The alarm on my phone went jangled, so I grabbed it off the nightstand and turned it off. The smell of coffee brewing and bacon made my mouth water. It had to be coming from the kitchen, which meant either my mother broke into my loft, or Georgia was here. Since my mother was allergic to cooking, it had to be Georgia, and I thought she had the day off.

I swung my feet to the floor, stood up, and squeezed my dick again. The bastard didn't want to go away, and since it had been a few weeks since Asher and I made love last, perhaps I'd better take matters into my right hand. I lay back on the bed, pulled my pajama bottoms down to my knees, and shut my eyes.

"Carter, I made you some breakfast."

"Damn it." I whispered. "Be there in a minute!" I called out, then forced myself out of bed. Well, that was definitely Georgia's voice, so at least the food would be good. I threw on my robe, then shut my eyes and remembered when I lifted a large rock in our yard and discovered slugs for the first time as a kid. The memory of that horrifying moment always worked as an erection killer. A few moments later, I grabbed my phone and typed out a quick message to Asher.

Good morning I love you

If Asher wanted to be courted, I'd court him. Maybe that's what had been missing in our relationship? The dots next to the message jumped for a moment, then Asher responded.

I love you more

"That felt good." I grinned. "I'll tell Asher at least once a day I love him." After connecting the charger to the phone, I went to the kitchen.

"Morning, Georgia." I grabbed a mug out of a cabinet and poured myself a cup of coffee. "I thought you had the day off?"

"Nope." She was in front of the stove with her back to me. "Sit, your breakfast is ready."

Georgia placed a plate filled with bacon, eggs, and sliced fruit in front of me after I sat. "I'm famished." I murmured, then put a napkin in my lap and dug in. "Asher and I stayed out late last night."

Georgia spun around, her mouth a perfect open circle. "Is that a good thing, or a bad thing?"

"It's an excellent thing." I slugged back half the coffee, and Georgia grabbed the coffee pot and topped my mug up. "We're getting married again, though we still have a lot of work to do on our relationship."

"Well now, that's wonderful news." She said, then gestured toward the chair across from me. "May I?"

"Yeah, fill a plate and sit."

She poured a cup of coffee and sat down. I loved her gray braids. They were so long she had to move them to make sure she didn't sit on the ends. "Does Florida know yet? Because she'll be so happy to know you're coming back to the family. She told me that everyone misses... hey, why didn't you sleep at the Yateses' house?"

I sighed, wishing I could have slept in my actual bed with Asher. "We're taking things slowly. But Asher says I can start planning the wedding. I've got a million things to do first." There was a pad of paper and a pen on the counter, so I grabbed them and sat back down.

1. Make an appointment with the wedding planner

2. Call Therapista

3. Personal shopper at Saks for Dior suits

4. Get new measurements taken of Asher. He's pushing maximum density, but I still love him.

"There. Those are the most important things." I tore off the paper and stuffed it in the robe. Mom would enter the note in my daily planner when I saw her later. "Sorry to eat and run, Georgia, but my day is packed, and I still haven't told Mom the good news."

Georgia lifted her coffee cup and an eyebrow. "Are you sure you want to be telling people yet? Like, maybe you should be one hundred percent sure before…"

"Everything's going to be perfect. I swear."

———

I arrived at work before Mom did and raced to my office to get ready for my first client. When I switched on the computer, I saw it was an Elizabeth Cole Robins, who wanted to expand her library. "Who the hell is, oh yes. The pharmaceutical empire." I'd already drawn up the plans, so I sent the file to the printer.

"Darling!" Mom poked her head in the door. "Have you

eaten already, because I was going to pop over to Baker's Treat and..."

"Sit!" I pointed at the chair in front of the desk. Once she was settled, I handed her the notes I'd taken at breakfast. "Please add these events to my calendar."

She glanced over it, and an enormous grin split her face. "Oh my baby boy, I'm so excited! But what happened to your date with Cort Tyler?"

"Yuck. Never mention that name to me again." I shook my head. "It was the date from hell, but Asher showed up with a fugly date of his own." Hmm. Mom was the only person who knew where we were going. "Did you tell Asher we were eating at L'Opossum?"

Mom's grin faltered. "Um, well," she shrugged. "Maybe?"

My mother was the mouth of the south. "Since it ended well, all is forgiven." I glanced at my watch and noted I had almost an hour before the Robins woman arrived. "Mom, give me that note back. I can take care of this stuff right now."

She handed me the paper. "Do you want me to grab you some breakfast while I'm at Baker's Treat?"

"Uh, no. Georgia already made me some."

Mom got to her feet. "Georgia? So you didn't spend the night with Asher?"

"No, we're taking things slowly. There's no way we can go back to the relationship we had without a little work. So, we're doing couples counseling, and, oh, let me do that now." I picked up the desk phone and punched in Therapista's number. Mom waved her fingers at me and left.

After setting up the appointment with her, I decided to tackle the other thing Asher wanted. Wooing.

I went to a florist's website and ordered six dozen roses to be delivered to Asher's office. Now what the hell would I put on the card? I'd barely scraped by in English class, so fancy poetry was out of the question.

Roses are red

Violets are blue

I suck at poetry Asher

But I still love you

"Well, that will have to do." I hit send on the order. "Hardly Shakespeare, but it gets the message across."

Afterward, I set up an appointment at Saks Fifth Avenue so they could fit us for our suits. Then I set a reminder to make an appointment with the wedding planner. Lori Stallings was the absolute best, and had planned most of our friends' weddings. Somehow, I had to make Mom and Asher's grandmother feel like they were contributing to the wedding plans. I was sure that Lori could figure something for them to do. Oh, and I couldn't forget Florida. It might be unorthodox to have the family maid in the wedding, but we were hardly a conventional family.

The phone rang, and after four rings, I remembered Mom was out getting breakfast.

"Camden Yates Interiors." I answered.

"Carter, this is Dr. Johnson's office. She wants to know if your appointment with her can be moved to a later time. It's for Monday afternoon at three, but we're hoping to make yours and Asher's appointment the last of the day, so she can spend more time with the two of you. Would 5:30 work?"

"Fine. Actually, that works better for us." I said and disconnected the call. Then a disturbing thought flew through my head.

"What if she discovers we're incompatible? Or, she messes with..." My gut clenched. Everything was still so raw. I knew Asher didn't want to see her. He lived his entire life in his head and rarely discussed his inner self with anyone but me or his family. Could he open up to anyone else?

CHAPTER 19

ASHER

"Now that the pandemic is over, many of our clients wish to continue virtual meetings instead of in-office ones. In my opinion, this is the future. What do you think, Asher?" Mom asked. We were in our weekly meeting with the partners, and this week we held it in my office. Noticeably absent was Cort, but since he was departing soon, it wasn't a big deal.

"I think it's an excellent trend, for many reasons."

Harry Minor, one of the founding partners, and our cousin, frowned. "Why is that good? As far as I'm concerned, we need to have private, one-on-one sessions with our clients in order to guarantee confidentiality. That's harder to do with virtual meetings."

Mom told me before the meeting that the old man was pissed off. Many of our staff now worked from home, and he was old school, wanting everyone in the office.

"There are many reasons to continue with virtual meetings. First, our clients genuinely like them. Customer satisfaction is more important than anything. Second, it will save us money in the long run." I opened my laptop and opened a file I'd created specifically for this meeting. Little bells rang from everyone's laptops as I shared it. All except for old cousin Harry, who hated computers.

"How on earth will virtual meetings save money?" Harry took a cigar from his pocket and put it in his mouth, unlit. Smoking wasn't allowed anymore, but he was from the old days, when they had ashtrays in department stores.

"Everyone, look at the file I just sent you." I asked. A moment later, I continued. "As everyone knows, we rent our office space from Morton G. Thalhimers. It's expensive, but we own a smaller office space in the Manchester neighborhood. That space is currently being rented from us by a medical billing service, and the lease is expiring in ten months. If we move into that space once their lease is up, we will save approximately 110k per month on rent."

"How can we fit our entire staff into that smaller space?" Harry asked.

"By allowing employees to work remotely, we don't need as much space." Mom rolled her eyes. She had little patience for the old man. "We already own that building, so let's use it."

I snuck a glance at my phone. Carter had been messaging me all day, each message telling me he loved me. Every single one of them brought tears to my eyes. When I told him I wanted to be wooed, he'd taken it seriously.

"But how can we monitor our associates if they aren't in the office?" Harry shook his head. "They'll spend all their time doing anything but working."

"Harry, in the file I shared, you can see that productivity increased during the pandemic, despite associates working from home."

"Honestly, Harry, I don't care what the associates are doing while working from home, as long as the job gets done." A lock of hair fell out of Mom's bun, and she slid it behind her ear. "According to our statistics, they not only did their work, but their quality of life increased. Happy associates make us more money."

"Excuse me." The door to my office opened, and my secretary poked her head inside. "Asher, I'm sorry to interrupt, but you've got a delivery, and it's too big to stay out here with me."

Mom shrugged her shoulders while Harry took an imaginary puff off his cigar. There were nine other partners at my conference table, and I wouldn't have much space here either. "Whatever it is, place it along the wall somewhere. There's not enough room."

"Yes sir." She opened the door, and a floral scent filled the air as a deliveryman carried a bouquet of red roses inside.

"Oh, how lovely." Mom smiled. "Put that in the middle of the table."

The deliveryman did as instructed, then he left without shutting the door. I knew these flowers were from Carter and I itched to read the attached card. Then, the man returned with another bouquet.

"You can put that one on my desk." I bit my lower lip to keep from giggling like a little boy. After placing it on my desk, he left and returned with another bouquet. Mom's eyebrows shot toward the ceiling, and Harry rolled his eyes.

"Excuse me sir," Mom asked. "How many bouquets are there?"

"Six."

"Oh my God." I murmured.

"Well now, why don't we adjourn this meeting until next week. Somebody is feeling the love today, and who are we to…" Mom began, and Harry cut her off.

"We need to settle this remote work thing because…"

"We need to let Asher enjoy his gifts." Mom shut her laptop

and stood. "Harry, I'll print the pertinent files off for you since you're allergic to technology. Read the material, and I guarantee you'll understand the proposal better at next week's meeting."

The delivery guy placed the last bouquet on my desk while everyone except Mother left my office. With trembling fingers, I opened the tiny envelope from the first bouquet.

"Are these from Carter?" Mom leaned over and sniffed the flowers.

"Yeah." I whispered, and I felt like my heart would burst out of my chest. "I'm, uh, he…"

"I'll leave you to enjoy these precious flowers in private." Mom pecked my cheek and turned toward the door. "Oh, why don't you invite Carter over to see the rest of us? We miss him terribly." She said over her shoulder, then shut the door quietly behind her.

I sat behind my desk and swiped at my eyes. "Carter, I love you so damned much." A tiny sob escaped, and I placed my face in my hands for a moment to calm down. This was exactly what I'd wished for. When Carter and I first started dating, it was me who always sent flowers, organized impromptu trips, and made grand romantic gestures. I always knew he loved me, but…

"Asher, Cort Tyler wants to speak to you." My secretary's voice spoke through the intercom. Damn it, what a buzzkill.

"Send him in."

The door opened and Cort's mouth fell open. "What is all this?"

"This is how Carter acts when he's in love." I winked, and a petty part of me enjoyed his discomfort. "To what do I owe this visit? I thought we'd already handed off your caseload to other associates."

"Well, I wanted to apologize for my actions. That isn't how friends should treat each other, and I'm hoping you'll forgive me." Cort's eyes dropped to his feet. I'd already forgiven him, because if he hadn't behaved the way he did with Carter, we might not be reconciled today.

"It's in the past, Cort. Is there anything else?"

"You're my favorite tennis partner, and I was hoping we could continue playing at the club together. Would you be up for it?" He lifted his gaze to mine. I might have forgiven him, but I'd be a fool to ever trust him again. There would be no further tennis dates with my former friend.

"Thanks for the invitation, but my weekends are full." I murmured, then without another word, Cort left. "Good riddance." I sat back down, and my cell phone buzzed. Glancing at the screen, I saw it was Carter.

"I love you." I said, my heart galloping in my chest.

"Ah, so you got the flowers." I could hear the smile in Carter's voice. "I woke up dreaming about you."

"Oh really?"

"I was hard as a rock, humping the mattress." He giggled, and suddenly my head was filled with images of Carter, naked underneath me. "It was tempting to take care of it myself, but…"

"Don't you dare." I growled. "My dick is hard just thinking of you jerking off. I want to watch you, then I'm going to—"

"Mom!" Carter yelped, and I realized he must be at work. Damn it, Sissy could ruin a wet dream. "Look, I need to go. Uh, something's come up."

I pressed down on my erection and moaned audibly into the phone.

"Oh God." Carter breathed. "I'll be right with you, Mom." I heard a door slam.

"Hey, speaking of overbearing mothers, mine wants to see you ASAP. Everyone misses you." I was tempted to unzip my slacks and jerk one out right now, but knowing my luck, someone would interrupt.

"Aww," Carter crooned. "I miss them too."

"Well, that settles it. Can you come by tonight?"

"Can we make it a sleepover?" Carter asked, and I resisted the urge to order him to stay the night. I wanted to claim him, make him shout my name while I made him come over and over again. But, despite my raging boner, we needed to take things slowly.

"Let's decide later tonight, after dinner." I sighed, then pressed down on my cock and groaned. Neither of us said anything, but I could hear his staggered breathing.

"I love you Asher. See you at seven." Carter breathed, then hung up.

CHAPTER 20

CARTER

"What's wrong with you today?" Mom asked when I entered the showroom. "One minute you're acting all moony over Asher, and the next you're practically tossing me out of your office."

I couldn't tell Mom that she had walked in on a sexy phone call with Asher. Mom and I were close, but not that close. "Sorry, Mom. I was dealing with a, um, frustrated client." I sighed and shook my head. That frustration would be over soon, I prayed. Asher and I had a wonderful sex life, but over the last few months it had dwindled down to almost nothing. It was a symptom of our problems, but hopefully we were on the mend and everything would go back to normal.

"Customers can be so picky about the stupidest things sometimes." Mom said, then handed me the mail. "These just arrived."

"Thanks." I muttered, glancing through them to see if any of it was important, but it was all junk and bills. "So, guess where I'm going tonight?"

"Is the club having an event? Or did you and Asher work things out enough to actually see each other again?"

"The latter." It took a major effort not to jump up and down like a ten-year-old. "I'm having dinner with Asher and the Yateses. I feel like I should bring something, but don't know what."

"Why? I mean, you live there, or at least you did." Mom said, whipping out a compact. She turned to the antique mirror behind the cash register and dusted her face with bronzer. "Actually, take something with you. A gift for Asher. Something romantic, don't you think?"

"I sent him several bouquets of roses today. Do you think more would be overkill?" I asked, then realized that when it came to romance, more was more. You couldn't overdo it, especially when we were working through our problems. Mom opened her mouth to reply, but I held my hand up. "I will bring him something. The question is, what?"

"I bet the Pink Cadillac has the perfect gift." Mom winked, referring to a store in the Cary Court shopping center. It sold bizarre clothes, and had a wonderful selection of cards and naughty novelty gifts. Hmm. Something for the bedroom would be perfect. "Do you want me to help you pick out a present?"

That's a big no. "Oh Mom, you stay here and mind the store. I'll be back in a few minutes."

———

"God, I hope this gift isn't too over the top for Asher." I flipped the turn signal and moments later I was on River Road, passing the Country Club of Virginia. Asher was a gifted lover, but he was a little conservative in the bedroom. I'd bought a game called Kinky Truth or Dare. When I was a kid I'd loved playing truth or dare, but not the spicy variety. Hopefully we'd be able to put it to use tonight.

"If he wants me to spend the night, that is." I sighed. I missed waking up in his arms, and the smell of his skin after we had sex. If he could bottle his musky scent, he'd make a fortune.

My heart pounded when I passed the Episcopalian retreat. The Yates estate was less than a mile away, and as much as I wanted to see Asher and the family, I was scared. What if things took a turn for the worse? I couldn't bear any more fighting, but I guess the only way for us to work through our issues was to confront them head on.

The brick wall surrounding the estate came into view, and when I pulled up to the gate, my fingers trembled as I punched in the code. I messed it up on the first try, and felt sweat dripping down my back. "Why the hell can't I get it right? Did they switch the code?" I pressed the buttons again, and the black metal gate slowly parted. "Thank God."

I passed through the gates only to find an enormous goose sitting in the middle of the driveway. "Shit." I muttered, and beeped the horn. Geese scared the hell out of me. When I was a little boy I'd been attacked by one who'd chased me around the algae-filled pond at Bryant park. The goose didn't move at first, so I pulled up closer to it and lowered the window.

"Get out of the way, you vile creature." I shook my fist at it, then heard a man laugh. It was one of the gardeners.

"I'll take care of it, sir." He boldly walked up to the bird and spoke in Spanish. The bird eyed me, then waddled away to the side of the pond where its flock were shitting all over the grass.

"Thanks." I rolled up the window and soon the house came into view. As a designer, I had to admit that the Yates house was the most stunning mansion on River Road. It was three stories tall, had 33 rooms, and took up 12,000 square feet. The perfect example of the American South during the gilded age, and it had been in the family for generations.

"It's a full house tonight." Mary Jane and Lila Brook's Bentley was parked next to Florida's minivan, so I pulled up next to it and cut the engine. I opened the car door, grabbed the gift, then thought better of it and left it in the seat. Who knew if I was spending the night or not? Plus, did I really want Asher to open this gift in front of his family?

The door to the tack room opened, and Asher strolled out with the biggest grin on his face. My heart melted, and I opened my arms. He walked into my embrace and squeezed me so tight I thought he'd crush my shoulders.

"Oh baby, you're a sight for sore eyes." His baritone voice filled my ear. "I could barely get any work done just thinking of seeing you tonight."

"I miss…"

"Carter!" Florida's voice rang out, and I reluctantly let go of my man. She crossed over to us, but instead of hugging me she hit my shoulder. "What the hell are you doing going out with other men? Nobody treats my boy that way." She put her arm around Asher's waist and frowned. This was a first. Normally she took my side in any argument.

"I'm truly sorry, Asher." I rubbed my shoulder. The tiny old woman was much stronger than she looked.

"You ever do anything like that again and I'll bend you over my knee and give you the punishment you deserve." She scowled, and I immediately thought of the gift and stared into Asher's blue eyes. Hopefully, a little spanking would happen later, but with Asher, not Florida.

"I promise to behave." This was directed at Asher, whose lips twitched.

"Dinner won't be ready for another hour, and Mrs. Yates is on an important phone call." Florida stood between us and looped her arms through ours and started walking us toward the house. "The ladies are dying to play cards, but one of you has to fill in for your mother until she's able to play."

At the back door she let go of us and led us single file through the tack room and into the kitchen.

"Oh, thank God." Asher's grandmother stood by the counter with a plate of brownies in one hand and a martini in the other. "Carter, it's lovely to see you again. Take these." She handed me the brownies. "I need you to play with me until my daughter gets off the phone. Come along." She ordered, and Asher and I followed her.

"Oh Carter, it's lovely to see you again." Lila Brooke smiled at me, but it wasn't the usual open grin I was used to. I glanced up at Asher, and was surprised to see his eyes squarely on me. He winked, then whispered, "They're all a little bent out of shape about Cort."

"Shit." I said aloud, and instantly regretted it.

"Don't use foul language." Granny sank into her seat and squinted at me.

"I'm very sorry." I replied, then sat across the table from her. "It's been awhile since I played bridge. Hopefully I'll…"

"I'm off the phone now." Marjorie strolled into the room wearing a peach colored gown with a matching turban.

"Are you having a Joan Crawford moment, Mom?" Asher cracked, and Marjorie walked over and kissed my cheek.

"I couldn't do anything with my hair, and since it's just us, I threw this on." Marjorie said, and I vacated the seat so she could play cards with the girls. Florida walked in while Mary Jane dealt the first hand.

"Florida, make me a drink please." Marjorie asked.

"Sure." Florida strolled around the table checking out everyone's cards, then went to the bar and started pouring a cocktail.

She handed Marjorie a whiskey on the rocks, then turned to everyone else. "Drinks, anyone?"

"I'll take an iced tea, unsweetened please." I replied, and all eyes focused on me. Hell, I wanted to spend the night in Asher's arms, not passed out in a drunken stupor.

"Florida, I would love a soda water with a wedge of lime." Asher said.

"What the hell?" Granny picked up a brownie. "You two are acting peculiar."

Asher put his arm around my shoulder. "We have plans for later, and don't want to get sloppy."

"I've never heard you sound so responsible in your life, darling." Marjorie winked at us. "How delightfully dull. Now, let's play cards."

For three hours we watched as the grand old ladies duked it out at bridge, and by the end of the evening Marjorie had to be helped to bed by Florida. Granny and her besties went down to the basement theater to rewatch the hippy movie Hair, leaving me and Asher alone.

Despite the fact we'd been with each other for years, now it felt different. All I wanted in a man was sitting next to me, and if he didn't want me to stay the night with him, I'd lose my mind. My palms were sweaty, my heart was pounding, and every time I opened myself to say something, the words vanished into thin air.

"So, did you enjoy seeing everyone again?" Asher asked, dipping his head while keeping his blue eyes locked on mine.

"Um, yeah." I licked my lips.

"They missed you. Well, except for Florida. She's a little

perturbed with you right now." Asher laid his hand on my knee, and my cock twitched.

"I was wrong all along." I muttered, my mouth suddenly dry. "About Cort and..."

"Shhh." Asher laid his index finger over my lips. "I know." He scooted closer to me, and laid his arm over my shoulder. "I've missed you, terribly."

"Oh?" Damn it, my heart was pounding so hard it almost felt like a panic attack.

"Hey, baby, relax. You're so stiff. It's just me, and..."

"Can I stay the night with you?" I blurted out, and Asher's eyes widened. "Please?"

CHAPTER 21

ASHER

"There's nothing I'd like more." I breathed. "But are you ready for it? Because we have a lot of stuff to work through, and..."

"Asher." Carter picked up my hand and held it against his chest. "Yes, we have a lot of work ahead of us, but you are the only man I've ever loved. I miss you."

It felt like something was stuck in my throat. I coughed, then stood up and held my hand out for Carter to take. "I walked here. Would you mind driving us back to the cottage?"

Carter grasped my hand, and I pulled him to his feet. "Yes, of course I'll drive."

Without letting go of his hand, we strolled through the house until we were in the kitchen. We were about to enter the tack room when Florida's voice drawled in the dark. "Y'all better be going home together."

We turned around, but couldn't see through the darkness. "We are." Carter's voice trembled, then we walked outside to Carter's black Mercedes, which was glowing in the moonlight. I opened the passenger door and sat.

"Ouch!" I'd sat on something square and hard. I pulled it out and saw it was a gift-wrapped box. After Carter settled into the driver's seat, I held it up so he could see it. "What's this?"

"Oh, that. It's a gift, kind of." Carter chuckled.

"For me?"

"Yes, it's for you. Actually, it's for both of us." Carter switched on the ignition and started inching down the driveway. "Wait until we get to the house before opening it."

"Carter. Do you remember when we used to dance together in the old boathouse?" I turned to watch his expression. A slow smile spread across his face. "Let's do it tonight. It's been so long since we danced together."

"I'd love to." Carter turned to me. "Aren't the lights broken in the boathouse? They were the last time we went down there.

"I want to hold you in the moonlight." I took his hand and squeezed it. "We can dance on the pier, or on the river bank. It honestly doesn't matter, as long as we are together."

Carter drove past the cottage, continuing until the end of the pavement. Once he switched the car off, we both got out of the car and I took his hand again. The moon was so bright that it was easy to see the dirt path leading to the boathouse.

"Oh shit, Carter. Your shoes might get messed up walking through the…"

"Doesn't matter. I'm the Imelda Marcos of Richmond and have plenty of shoes to spare." He grinned, then he pulled me forward. The path used to be a tiny road where my grandparents would pull their boats to the river, and the landscapers still kept it clear. A few moments later, we could hear the low roar of the rapids.

"How long has it been?" Carter squeezed my hand. "Two years?"

"Yes, something like that." It felt so right being with him, and when the James river came into sight, we both stopped in our tracks.

"God, it's so beautiful." Carter murmured. "Why did we stop coming down here?"

I knew the answer, and it was an uncomfortable truth we both needed to face. "Because we were always hanging out with the wackadoos up at the main house. They like to drink and party, and we fell into a routine of doing the same. By the time the partying ended for the night, we were too wasted to even consider dancing in the moonlight."

"Oh, yeah." Carter's voice hitched. "You know I love your family, but maybe we spent too much time with them."

"Maybe we spent too much time drinking with them." I bit off the last few words. Ever since our relationship soured, the suspicion that we were partying too much had grown within me.

"Maybe." Carter whispered, then we stared out at the river for a long moment, saying nothing. The moon was perfectly reflected in the water, which appeared blue in the moonlight, despite being a muddy brown. There was a tiny island in the middle of the water, and it had a tree with tiny flowers softly glowing white in the night.

"Remember when we first got married, and you'd wanted us to buy a house somewhere else, Asher?"

I dropped his hand and fished my phone out of my pocket. "Yes. And I still think it's a good idea. But I know how much you love the cottage, and I don't want us to make any rash decisions. Plus, the ladies are getting older. Us being nearby is probably a good thing." I found a romantic playlist online and turned on the music. After setting the phone down on a nearby rock, I bowed before Carter and held my hand out. "May I have this dance?"

Carter said nothing, just stared at me a moment before

taking my hand. I pulled him into my chest, and we started swaying to a Madonna song, Crazy For You. "I love this song." Carter breathed, then began humming along to it.

My hands dropped to Carter's waist, and I tightened our embrace. This felt so right, having him in my arms. My pulse ticked up, and euphoria raced through my body. God, this was so much better than an alcohol and magic brownie fueled evening with my family. If they could bottle up the intense emotions I was feeling now and sell it to the world, we'd be billionaires millions of times over.

"Love is the drug." I whispered in Carter's ear, and I felt him trembling. "Nothing is better than this, my love."

Carter stopped moving, then looked up at me. "Do you feel it too? Like, what we have is the best thing on the planet, and all we've done is mess things up by being stupid?"

I sighed. "We are stupid. But I'd rather be stupid with you than ever be away from your side again."

"I love you." Carter whispered, and our feet slowly began to move again. "I love you more than all this, the beautiful homes and luxuries. If I had to give it all up just to be by your side, I would in a heartbeat."

The song changed, and Endless Love by Diana Ross and Lionel Richie began. Carter squeezed me even tighter, and I thought I heard a small sob come from him.

"This should be our song, because it's how I feel about you, Asher. A love so enormous it fills the sky, from one horizon to the other." Carter's voice was thick, and a tear slipped down my cheek.

"I love you too, Carter. For now and for always. Now, will you do me the honor of coming home with me? To our home?"

"Wherever you are is home for me."

CHAPTER 22

CARTER

We strolled back to my car, and Asher sat on the silly gift I got for us again.

"Ouch." He moved forward and pulled the box out from behind him. "So, what is this gift for?"

Suddenly, I felt embarrassed by it. The moment by the river had been magically romantic. Did I want to spoil the mood with some pointless sex game? But there was no getting away from it now. "You can open it when we get back to the cottage." I started the car, and we headed back up the driveway. "It's nothing important. Actually, it's quite silly."

Asher laid his hand on my knee, and a couple of minutes later, I pulled up in front of the cottage and cut off the engine. Asher and I got out of the car, and a smile split my face. This was home, where I wanted to spend the rest of my life with Asher.

When I opened the door and turned on the overhead light in the kitchen, Asher began tearing at the gift wrapping. Seconds later, he was staring at the box with a look of amusement stamped on his face. "Kinky Truth or Dare? This is going to be fun." He waggled his eyebrows, then took my hand and dragged me up the stairs to our bedroom. Asher threw open the door, then launched himself on the bed and opened the box.

"Hmm, so I want to go first." He toed off his shoes and let them drop to the floor. "Truth or dare, Carter."

I perched on the side of the bed and took off my shoes. "Truth." I wasn't quite prepared for any dares yet.

Asher picked a card and read from it. "What do you remember about the first time you had sex?"

I giggled, then started unbuttoning my shirt. "It was awful. Me and this girl named Douglas, who is a very masculine lesbian, had our first time experience with each other. Neither of us knew, or would admit to being gay. Honestly, it was all one big fumble in the dark. I didn't get off, and she didn't either. But what made it interesting is that we did the deed at Lakeside Presbyterian Church." I reached for the box and pulled a card out. "Your turn Asher. Truth or dare."

"You did it with a lesbian inside a church? Damn, you're kinkier than I thought. Truth."

I read the question and blushed. "Give me another card. I don't like this one."

"No baby, just read it. I promise not to think any less of you. Hell, these might be questions we should've answered a long time ago." Asher nudged me with his foot. I sighed, then read the question.

"Would you ever want to watch me have sex with someone else?"

"Hell no." Asher frowned. "Why on earth would I want to do that?"

"I was just reading the question." Inwardly, I was pleased at his answer. "Your turn." I stood and pulled my shirt off, then unzipped my slacks.

"Truth or dare, Carter."

I still wasn't ready for a dare. "Truth."

Asher giggled. "Where is the strangest place you've ever masturbated?"

"Oh, God." I pulled my pants off, then settled next to Asher on the bed. "In a bathroom stall at church. The sermon bored me, so I told Mom I had to go to the bathroom, and jerked off until the service was over."

"You have a church kink." Asher lifted his ass off the mattress and pulled his slacks down, then kicked them to the floor. "Would it turn you on if I dressed up like a priest or something?"

"God no. There's a reason I'm an atheist. Truth or dare, Asher." I took the box of cards from him and pulled one out.

"Truth."

"Are you too chicken for a dare?" I asked, then eyed the card. Actually, I was glad he wanted to play truth, because the dare was way too extreme for both of us.

"No, but I'm working up the courage. Now go on, read the question." He leaned into me, trying to read the card.

"What's the kinkiest thing you've ever done?" I slid the card back in the box and waited for him to answer.

"Hm. I'm kind of vanilla, so..." Asher shut his eyes for a moment, then he answered the question. "Back in college, me and this guy had a friends with benefits thing going on. Nothing serious, but he loved to be tied up. So, I guess that's the kinkiest thing I've done. How about you?"

"Do you have to ask? Me and the church have a sordid history." I giggled. Asher pulled a card out of the box, and I decided to spice things up.

"Truth or dare Carter."

"Dare." My pulse ramped up. We were lying next to each

other wearing only our briefs, and it was high time they came off.

"Ah, finally, we're gonna see some action." Asher winked. "Show me the last porn video you watched."

"Oh God." I rarely watched porn, but during our brief separation, I'd watched a few videos. "Fine." I reached down and snagged my pants from the floor, and pulled my phone out. A moment later, I found it and handed the phone to Asher. "I don't know the title, but the girl is funny as hell."

"Girl? Are you secretly bisexual?" Asher hit play on the video, and I snuggled next to him to watch.

"No. But this video has real acting in it, so it's a little more entertaining." I wrapped my arm around his waist and laid my head on his chest.

Two men were in a restaurant kitchen fucking, while a waitress kept bringing them more orders. They were behind a counter, and while it was obvious they were screwing, she couldn't figure out why her orders weren't being made. Frustrated that they weren't working, despite the copious amount of sweat coating the two guys, she finally rushes inside and catches them in the act.

Asher laughed aloud at the woman's face when she caught them. Her mouth was comically wide open, and her eyes looked like they were bugging out of her head. I started laughing with him, then he stopped and eyed me. "Are you secretly an exhibitionist? Because you like doing it in places where you could get caught."

Hm. I'd never thought of that. "Maybe?" I snatched a card out of the box. "Truth or dare, Asher."

"If you can do it, so can I." Asher bit his lower lip, then answered, "Dare."

I read the dare to myself and licked my lower lip. "Demonstrate your oral sex technique using the nearest appropriate object."

"Yes sir." Asher murmured, then he scooted down until his face was over my now erect cock. Without asking, he pulled my briefs down and tossed them to the floor. Then he lifted my cock to his lips and licked the head. I groaned, then he took it in his mouth.

"Oh yes." I hissed, and Asher went further down my shaft, licking and teasing. Suddenly, he let go of my cock and looked up at me. "Could we try one of my fantasies out?"

"If it involves me getting the best head of my life, I'm all in." I breathed, and Asher got off the bed and pulled his briefs down. Then he went to the closet, walked inside, and returned holding a handful of neckties. "What are you going to do with those?"

"Get in the middle of the bed, spread eagle."

His voice had a commanding edge to it that made my cock throb. After doing what he asked, he tied my wrists to the headboard, then did the same with my feet at the foot of the bed. "Bondage, sweetheart?" I never once imagined he was into that kind of stuff. A shiver went up and down my spine as he leered down at my naked body.

"Now, where were we?" Asher lay on top of me, his lips inches from mine. My mouth opened, and his lips crashed into mine. His groan went into my mouth, along with his tongue. My cock felt so hard it almost hurt. He ground his shaft into mine, then he abandoned my lips and began licking the side of my neck. My arms strained against the ties, and my skin felt so sensitive I squirmed and moaned beneath him.

"Oh my God," I breathed. Asher moved further south, and he licked underneath my armpit, then he began kissing the tender skin of my sides. Once again, my arms and legs strained to be free, and I gasped. Never in my life had I trusted anyone to restrain me, and my breathing became hitched, all the while making noises I'd never made before. "This is so intense."

By now Asher was at my waist, and he removed his mouth from my skin and blew a stream of warm air on my throbbing shaft.

"Please, Asher, take me in your mouth." My hips were bucking, so Asher placed a hand on each hip and held me in place. Then he took my cock in his mouth again. "Oh Jesus," I panted, wondering how a simple blow job could make me into a whimpering fool.

Asher began moving his mouth up and down my shaft, and despite his hands holding me in place, my hips bucked, trying to get more of me into his warm mouth. He let go of my left hip and wrapped his fingers around the base of my shaft. Using his hand and his mouth, he sucked my cock, and I could feel my come being pulled out of me. "Asher, you've never, ever, oh my god, I'm so close." I breathed, and suddenly, he let my cock fall out of his mouth and it hit my stomach with a loud thwack. "Please, don't stop now!" I thrashed underneath him, a tiny sob vibrating through my chest.

"Now we get to do something I've always wanted to do." Asher peered down at me, then reached into the nightstand and pulled out the bottle of lube. He was so rakish, with a dark-blond curl falling into his eyes as he poured the thick gel into his palm. Then he coated my shaft with it and started climbing on top of me.

"What the hell are you doing?" I gasped. "Aren't you a virgin?" Asher once told me he'd never been fucked before, and since I loved the feel of his girth inside me, I'd never insisted on topping him. Asher brushed his hair out of his eyes, then positioned the head of my cock against his entrance. He moved it back and forth against his hole, while never losing eye contact.

"Yes, but you're the only man I've ever wanted to fuck me." Asher lowered himself on to me, and winced. "You've never fucked a man before either, right?"

I felt the head of my cock break through his tight ring, and I gasped. "I guess we're both losing our virginity tonight."

CHAPTER 23

ASHER

Carter was a healthy boy downstairs, and when the head of his cock entered me, my eyes snapped shut. Stars floated behind my eyelids, and for a moment I forgot to breathe, but it was worth it. I had to prove to Carter how much I loved him, and make myself vulnerable to him, too.

"You're so tight." Carter hissed, and I lowered myself onto his cock a little more. Carter's hands grabbed my waist. My eyes opened, and Carter's eyes were shut, his lips stretched into a dopey smile. I wished it felt that good for me, but there had to be a reason guys enjoyed getting fucked. Hopefully, I'd find out soon, because right now it just hurt. "I never thought you'd let me fuck you, and man, it feels awesome." Carter whispered, and I lowered myself a little more and winced.

When does this start feeling good?

Without warning, Carter thrust his hips up, and a bolt of pain shot through me.

"Damn it!" I yelled, then sank all the way down on his thick shaft. At least this way he couldn't surprise me again. "Please, don't move." My voice sounded ragged, and my heart was pumping so hard I wondered if I was about to faint.

"Are you okay?"

I looked down, and Carter's tan cheeks were flushed. "Yeah, just let me get used to your size. Jesus, Carter. You feel so huge inside me, and…"

"Oh, you think I have an enormous cock, Daddy?" Carter bit his lower lip, and if I wasn't in so much pain, I'd have laughed. Of course, I'd said the right thing. Tell any man he was well-hung and he'd light up like a Christmas tree.

"Yeah, baby. I never realized how big until it was inside me." I struggled to catch my breath.

"Asher, if this doesn't feel good we don't have to…"

"No, I want this, more than anything." I wheezed.

"Get off me." Carter commanded, his voice sounding much more butch than I was used to. "Get off me now, and lie down on your back next to me."

"Yes, sir." I did as he ordered, and oddly enough, I felt empty when his girth slid out of me. Carter got on his side and kissed my nipple. Then he got on top of me and slid down my body until his mouth hovered over my now soft cock. He took the head in his mouth, then I felt his fingers rubbing my entrance. "This feels awesome."

My eyes shut, and one of his fingers slid inside of me. After having his sizable cock in me, it slid in with ease. "Oh yeah, now that feels fantastic." His finger kept hitting this spot inside of me that felt odd, yet amazing at the same time. Couple that with his expert oral skills, and my dick firmed up. Then I felt a second digit slide inside, and I felt my muscles tightening around his fingers. A moment later, I relaxed, and when his fingers hit that spot again, I felt something inside me spasm in an excellent way.

For the longest time, I'd always thought of Carter as a do-me-queen. We'd had a good sex life, but it was always the same thing. I'd get him warmed up with a little oral action, then I'd fuck him. When he got off, that was when I would allow myself to come. I had to admit, I was loving the change of pace. In fact, if he kept on working my cock and ass at the same time, I was going to shoot my load before we went any further.

Carter's tongue swirled around my cockhead at the same time his finger touched that spot again, and a low groan came from deep within my chest. Carter froze, then his fingers slid out of me and his mouth let go of my cock.

"No, please, I was almost..."

"It's time to experience pleasure, Asher. Trust me, my fingers feel great, but now you're going to find out how amazing it feels with me fully inside you." Carter's voice was so different, so commanding. God, it was totally turning me on. Like, had he always been like this and just hadn't bothered to show me?

Carter got in-between my legs and placed my legs over his shoulders. Then he grabbed the bottle of lube and slicked up his cock some more. "Asher, I love you."

His words filled my ears, and I wanted him inside me now. "I love you too." I whispered, then felt the head of his cock pushing against my entrance.

"Relax, baby." Carter's voice deepened as his dick breached my entrance, and to my relief, it didn't hurt. He pushed in more, and I made a noise I'd never made before in my life. It was the lowest, deepest groan, like something out of a porn film. "Open your eyes Asher."

I did as he ordered and almost forgot to breathe. His warm brown eyes were focused on me, and a single tear snaked down the side of his nose. He pushed inside deeper, hitting that spot, and I groaned again.

"Yes, that's it baby." Carter smiled, then he pulled most of his shaft out before plunging in to the hilt. My back arched, and I held on to his forearms as he once again pulled almost all the way out, then hammered his cock back inside me. This man, the man I loved with all of my heart, was finally making love to me in a way that made the world disappear. It was just Carter and me, and I never wanted it to stop.

He stopped moving for a minute, and I noticed a sheen of sweat covering his face and chest. Then he leaned down and brushed his lips across mine. "Are you ready?"

"Ready for what?" I breathed, and a drop of Carter's sweat dripped from his nose, hitting my lips.

"For this." Carter snarled, and he began hammering in and out of me so fast I couldn't think. Soon the headboard was slamming against the wall, and Carter's hand gripped my cock. I'd never seen him like this before, so commanding and so masculine. He jerked my cock while pounding me, and I felt pressure building in my groin.

"I can't believe it, I'm going to come, Carter, swear to God I'm, oh, I'm…" Carter pushed in all the way just as come flew out of my cock, painting my stomach and chest.

"Yes!" Carter shouted, then he went still, and I felt his cock spasm. His entire body shook, and I felt heat inside of me. A moment later, he collapsed. His cock slipped out of me as he pasted himself to my come-and-sweat-slicked torso, struggling to catch his breath.

We lay like that for a long moment, panting while our sweaty bodies slowly returned to normal. I felt his lips against the side of my neck, and realized he was murmuring I love you, over and over again.

"I love you too," I whispered. "Nobody else but you, Carter."

"I don't wanna go." I heard Carter murmur as he wrapped his body around mine. My eyes fluttered open to see the morning sun rising through the window.

"You don't want to go where?" I asked, then I felt his warm lips against the back of my neck.

"To work." He sighed, then pulled me in closer to him. "I have an early appointment with the Southall woman down the street. She's paying me extra to start the work at her house a week early. The contractors had an opening, so I booked them."

"Asher! Carter!"

We froze at the sound of Florida's voice.

"Your Mama wants you two to come to breakfast at the big house." She was downstairs, and knowing her, she'd cleaned the kitchen instead of allowing her niece to do it.

"Be there in a few minutes!" Carter yelled, and a moment later, we heard the door to the kitchen shut behind her. Carter sat up and turned to me.

"Damn it. Why did we move into this cottage again?"

CHAPTER 24

ASHER

"We have to make this fast." Carter said as we got out of our cars. We both drove since I had to go to the office, while he had work too. Thankfully, Lila Brooke and Mary Jane's Bentley wasn't here, so we only had to deal with family.

When we entered the house, my stomach growled. Whatever Florida had cooked smelled amazing. As soon as we entered the kitchen, she ran up and gave me a hug, then gave Carter the side eye.

"What? No hug for me?" Carter tilted his head toward her.

"Not until you're legally married again. Gotta make sure you're not sleeping around behind Asher's back." She shooed us out of the kitchen, and when we reached the dining room, Granny was at the table alone.

"Where's Mother?" I pulled out a seat, then opened the newspaper next to it. Carter sat next to Granny, who beamed at him.

"Marjorie will be down any minute. So, you spent the night together." She winked. "Does that mean I can..."

"Darlings, it's lovely to see you two smiling again." Mother strolled in wearing a charcoal-gray power pantsuit. She only wore them when she had to appear in court. Mom said she was sick of lawyers and judges paying more attention to her legs than to her arguments. I think she got the idea from Hillary when she ran for president. They were old friends, and Mom had helped with her campaign in Virginia. "So, what's on your agenda today?"

Carter rolled his eyes. "Beverly Southall from down the street. She hounded me to get her job done early, so as soon as I'm done eating, I'm driving over to make sure the contractor gets everything right."

"Ew. Beverly, that stuck up woman. Does she still have that bottle-blonde bouffant?" Granny shook her head. "The woman has had the same hairstyle since 1972."

"Yes, it's an unfortunate look, Mother." Mom said, then Florida entered the room, pushing a cart full of food. She placed a frosted glass in front of Mom, and God only knew what was in it. Florida then heaped my plate full of pancakes, sausage, and a biscuit smothered in gravy. She didn't bother with Carter's plate. I glanced over at him, and he was suppressing a grin. It was nice being in Florida's good graces for a change.

"As I was saying earlier, now that things are better between the two of you, Asher, can we plan a wedding?" Granny eyed me, then turned to Carter. He shrugged his shoulders.

"I guess so?" I shrugged my shoulders too. We hadn't mentioned the wedding in a while, and though we were working through our problems, I decided to let Carter deal with the marriage question.

"Neither of you sound enthusiastic." Mom sipped her drink, and a suspicious flush raced up her neck. I would definitely drive her to the office. "I have another date with Judge Gottwald after work. He's taking me to the Dominion Performance Center to see a production of Madame Butterfly. It's my favorite opera."

"I want to help plan your wedding!" Granny shouted, taking us all by surprise. She reached up and fiddled with her hearing aid, then shook her head. "You're my only grandchild, Asher, and Marjorie has too much on her plate as it is. I know you have no interest in planning it, so Carter, myself, and the girls will plan the event of the season."

"My mother insists on helping too." Carter winked at me, and Granny scowled. She knew she couldn't exclude Sissy, but she'd try her best. Honestly, I liked my mother-in-law, though she could be a little over the top. "Why don't we start planning it tonight? Invite Lila Brooke and Mary Jane over, and I'll bring Mother."

Mom eyed Granny, who sighed dramatically. Granny didn't hate Sissy so much as she resented having to spend time with her. I secretly believed it was because she and the girls felt uncomfortable partying around Carter's mother. Once Sissy left, they'd get shitfaced.

"I'll call the event director at the country club and invite her over, too." Granny tilted her head in Carter's direction. "Well, that settles it. It's time to see you boys properly married."

———

"Have a wonderful day at the office." Carter pecked me on the cheek, then did the same to Mother.

"Don't let Beverly bully you. She's such a busybody." Mom opened the door to my Jaguar. "How Randall puts up with her is beyond me." She referred to Beverly's husband, the long-suffering president of the lung association. "I don't know how late I'm going to be, so play bridge without me." She grinned at both Carter and me and got into the car.

"I'll see you tonight." I glanced into the car to see if Mom was looking. Then I nuzzled Carter's neck. "Want a repeat of last night after the wedding planning is done?"

"Stop, or I won't be able to get any work done." Carter bit his lower lip and stared into my eyes. "I love you."

"I love you too." I reluctantly let go of him and got in the front seat. Mom was using my mirror to apply makeup. While waiting for her to be done, Carter drove off.

"Well, you boys seem to be getting along much better." Mom brushed a coat of mascara on her eyelashes, then tossed the tube in her purse.

"How are you going to the opera straight from work? You're hardly dressed for it." I adjusted the mirror and started the car.

"Oh darling, young people mostly do stupid things, but one lovely thing they've done is make everything so casual." She laughed. "The last time I was at the symphony, half of the audience was wearing blue jeans. Trust me, my pantsuit is just fine."

I turned out of the driveway, and a moment later we passed the Southalls' home. Carter was getting out of his car, and Beverly was shaking her hands dramatically in the air. Mom waved, and Beverly's mouth dropped open. She was a social climber, and Mom was the queen of Richmond society.

"You just made that woman's day." I chuckled, and Mom clucked her tongue.

"She's so pretentious. Thank goodness you can't see our house from the road. They should build a wall around the property." Mom patted my knee. "So, how did things go with Carter last night?"

I blushed.

"That good, huh?" Mom laughed. "Fine, I don't need details. So, about the wedding."

"What about it?"

"I watched you back at the house, and when Mother

brought up the wedding plans, you didn't react." Mom's phone buzzed. She glanced at it, then dropped it in her briefcase. "Just a short time ago, you confessed to me you wished that you and Carter would just shack up. Are you prepared for a society wedding, and all the scrutiny it brings with it?"

"Mom, I will do anything Carter wants." I gestured toward the green golf course surrounding the Country Club of Virginia on my left. "We'll be the first gay couple to be married there. I kind of like the idea of breaking that taboo. Plus, if it makes Carter happy, I'm all for it."

"What about the money? You insisted that Carter keep the costs reasonable, and if I'm any judge of character, Carter's incapable of having a low-key wedding." Mom was always a lawyer, arguing both sides to make sure you knew what you wanted.

"Carter's making excellent money at his design firm." I sighed. "He'll help cover the costs. Though I hope he doesn't go overboard. It's not the money I'm worried about, it's the specta-cle. If I had my way, we'd go to the justice of the peace, but if Carter's happy, and the rest of you, I'll do whatever he wants."

Traffic slowed at the Libbie Avenue intersection, and Mom shook her head. "When we pass this mess..." She waved her hands at the line of cars waiting to turn. "... take the downtown expressway. I have to be in court this morning, and I can't be late."

"Of course." I said, hoping she'd drop the subject of the wedding. Hell, Carter and I'd barely talked about the new cere-mony. All I wanted was for us both to be happy.

"You mentioned a civil ceremony, in front of a justice of the peace." Mom rested her hand on my forearm for a moment. "Have you ever thought that you should follow your heart? Ever since you were a baby, you were quiet, and you hated society functions. The spotlight doesn't shine naturally on you."

Mom shrugged. "Have you ever thought Carter is the one who should bend a little?"

"But, Mom, he already did. When we were originally married, it was very low-key." I grinned at the memory. "On the mountain, just us and that incompetent woman. Now, it's Carter's turn. He can do whatever he wants."

"But darling, is marriage what you really want?" Mom's tone turned sharp. "I'll drop the subject. But I want you to reflect on the life you and Carter have shared. You are the one who does most of the compromising. Are you prepared to spend the rest of your life playing second fiddle to Carter?"

CHAPTER 25

CARTER

"Mom, can you come over to the Yates estate tonight?"

The bottle of water Mom just pulled from the mini-fridge in my office clattered to the floor. Thank goodness the lid was on.

"Why?" Mom leaned over and picked it up. "They hate me."

"No, Mom, they don't." I sighed. Obviously I couldn't tell the truth, that while they didn't hate her, they wanted to spend as little time as possible with her. "Things are working out with Asher, and we're planning the wedding. I need your help."

"Really?" Mom sat on the other side of my desk. "What's been happening? I mean, what's changed with you and Asher?"

I couldn't tell her the X-rated version, so I settled for PG-13. "We spent a very romantic evening together, and have been communicating more honestly about our, um, desires. Now, his family wants an enormous wedding at CCV." I said, referring to the country club's initials. "If I don't have you there planning this event with me, Asher's grandmother and her girlfriends will put themselves in charge. With you by my side, it will be harder for them to do it."

"Okay." Mom brushed a lock of dark hair off her forehead. "I understand that, but I just feel so uncomfortable around them. Isn't there a way I could help from the sidelines? They're very intimidating."

"Mom, don't let them scare you off." I leaned across my desk and whispered. "Promise not to say a word of what I'm about to tell you."

"Of course, Carter." She leaned forward. "I promise not to utter a word."

"They don't hate you. But, I think the reason for their attitudes whenever you are around is because you aren't, well, as much of an alcoholic as they are." I said, and Mom's mouth opened into a perfect O. "They feel like they can't party with you around."

"But... but, that's ridiculous." Mom spluttered. "I party every once in a while."

"Mom. The ladies are embarrassed, because when I say they party, they really party." I grinned. "Like, if they were a 1970s rock band, they would leave destroyed hotel rooms in their wake. Asher and I tried to keep up with them, but we can't." It was the truth. Whenever we stayed up late with the ladies, we were always the first ones to pass out. They all had livers of iron, well, except for Mary Jane. She was the group stoner.

"So, do I need to become a raging alcoholic like Marjorie in order to fit in with them?" Mom's eyebrows shot up, and I glanced away. You could see straight up her nose.

"No, but..." I drummed my fingers on my desk. "...if you could loosen up a little, it would help. I've got an idea. Why don't you leave your car here and drive with me to their house after work. Plan on taking an Uber home. And if you feel like drinking a little bit more than usual, you won't have to worry about getting into an accident. Actually, why don't you plan on spending the night with me." I pointed at my chest. "You know, Mom, if you ever wanted to move upstairs, I'd be all for it. It would be nice to know someone was always here."

"No, to that." Mom sipped her water. "I love my little house. But I'll spend the night with you." Mom stood and went to the floor-to-ceiling mirror next to the mini-fridge and stared at her reflection. "Is this outfit okay, or will they laugh at me behind my back?"

They were going to judge the hell out of her, no matter what she wore. "Mom, you look wonderful." I walked over and hugged her from behind. "You are a stunning woman, and don't allow your fears of the Yates family to hold you back. Just relax a little when you're around them. I'm more worried about Lori Stallings."

"Who's that?"

"She's the event coordinator for CCV." I sighed. "Granny spoke with her on the phone earlier about coming by tonight to plan the wedding. Normally it takes months to get an appointment with her, but as soon as she heard it was the Yates, she…"

"Dropped everything and insisted on starting the wedding preparations immediately." Mom sighed. "I wish I had that kind of pull. Must be nice being a member of that family."

"Mom, I want you to remember that you are, by extension, a member of the Yates family. Don't let them or anyone else push you around."

———

"Carter, you should bring your mother over more often." Florida hugged Mom, who stood stock still with her hands at her sides. "It's good to see you again, Mrs. Camden. And as for you," Florida pointed at me. "...You'd better be on your best behavior."

Florida let go of Mom and went to work chopping vegetables on the granite kitchen island.

"Mom, let's go into the living room. We're a little early, so let's get you a drink to loosen you up." I took Mom's hand and dragged her out of the kitchen. No one was in the living room yet, but I could hear voices coming from upstairs. "What would you like to drink, Mom?"

"Water."

"Mom," I put my hands on my hips. "I know you don't feel like drinking, but..."

"Wine then." Mom shook her head and settled onto the pink velvet love seat. "I love the interiors. Have you done any of this work, Carter?"

"Oh no." I poured Mom and me a glass of Cabernet and sat next to her. "The furniture and accessories have been in the family for generations. Honestly, I don't see the need to change anything. It's perfect as is."

"Thank you for saying that, Carter." Granny strolled into the room. Her platinum bob was perfectly styled, and she had on the major jewels. Probably as an intimidation tactic with Mom and Lori Stallings. It surprised me her left bicep wasn't as big as a bodybuilder given the size of the emerald on her middle finger. "Mrs. Camden, it's nice to see you again." Granny murmured, and Mom stood and held her hand out. Granny eyed it for a moment, then shook it once and let it drop.

"Please, call me Sissy." Mom grinned, and Granny did a double take before sitting across from us. She must have noticed the new nose.

"Lila Brooke and Mary Jane should be here any minute now. Oh, and Lori Stallings is running a few minutes behind. Would you like a, oh sorry. You already have a drink. I'm feeling a little thirsty myself." Granny tottered over to the bar and poured herself a drink. When she sat down across from us, an unreadable smile spread across her face.

"Hi!" Mary Jane called out when she and Lila Brooke strolled into the room. She placed a silver platter in the center of the coffee table filled with chocolates. "I just whipped these up last night." She peeled off a layer of plastic wrap and stuffed it in the pocket of her calf-length kelly green skirt. "There's salted peanut, strawberry peppercorn, and, for purists like myself, dark chocolate truffles."

"I'm thirsty." Lila Brooke sauntered over to the bar and fixed herself a martini, and grabbed a bottle of water for Mary Jane. Mom eyed me, confused. She thought all the ladies were drunks. I'd tell her after the meeting about Mary Jane being a stoner. "Lord, it's been forever since I've been to a good wedding. Most of them are deadly dull." Lila Brooke settled next to Mary Jane, then ate the olive from her martini. "We're making sure this is the wedding of the year."

The doorbell rang, startling me. Nobody ever used the front door unless they weren't related. It must be the wedding planner.

"Asher, go sit with the ladies. I'll get the door." I heard Florida from the kitchen. Asher strolled in, kissed the top of my head, then sat on the other side of Mom.

"Why are you here, Asher? We know you aren't interested in planning a wedding." Lila Brooke asked.

"Hi, Sissy," Asher tilted his head and smiled. Mom pecked him on the cheek, then wiped off the lipstick print. Florida walked past us toward the front door. "I'll leave most of the planning up to Carter, but I want to keep informed about the upcoming ceremony."

"Is your mother coming, Asher?" Mom asked, even though she knew she wouldn't be here. I guessed she was trying to make conversation. Then I noticed her smoothing down her skirt, repeatedly, like a nervous tic.

"No, mother is attending the opera this evening. But she might show up later, depending on how well her date goes." Asher stood. "Excuse me, Sissy, I'm going to make myself a drink. Do you need anything?" His gaze moved back and forth between me and Mom. Both of us shook our heads no. A moment later, he returned with a glass of wine.

"Miss Lori Stallings." Florida announced, and we all stood up. In walked a tall blonde amazon wearing head-to-toe Prada. Her hair was pulled back in a tight bun, and following behind her was a mousy girl lugging sample books, fabric swatches, and a briefcase.

"How is everyone?" The woman flashed a toothy smile, then gestured for everyone to be seated. Well, except for her assistant. She pointed at the stuff the girl was carrying and said, "Put those next to me, then you can wait outside until I need you. Thanks, Mindy." She sat in the mint-green-velvet wing-back chair and smiled. "Well now, this is going to be the most talked about wedding in the Country Club of Virginia's history." The girl dropped everything next to the chair and hurried out of the room.

"Miss Stallings, would you like something to drink?" Granny asked.

"Usually I stick to water, but since this is my last appointment of the day, a glass of red wine would be delightful." Her eyes landed on the chocolates, and her face lit up. "Ooh, I would love some chocolate."

Mary Jane beamed at her. "They're homemade."

"Even better. After the day I've had, I'm sure they'll hit the spot." She rose from her chair, filled a napkin with a few of the treats, and sat again. Granny passed a glass of merlot to her, then we all waited for her to settle in. She bit into a truffle, and moaned. "This has to be the best chocolate I've ever had!"

"I was going to eat these a little later, but why wait?." Mary Jane filled a napkin, then to my surprise, Mom did too. She probably didn't want to stand out for not eating them. I tried one, and so did Asher, and soon everyone was oohing and ahhing about how yummy they were. After they had a chance to nibble on the treats, Lori got down to business.

"Congratulations Asher and Carter. From what I understand, you already were married, but there was a mixup. With me in charge, have no fear. My weddings always go off without a hitch." She sipped her wine, then continued. "Before we go any further, I want you to know that the board of the country club is fully behind your wedding. We've strived to become more inclusive and diverse, and everyone wants this to be a showstopper wedding."

"Thanks." I nodded my head.

"When you say showstopper, what exactly do you mean?" Asher crossed his arms over his chest. Hopefully, he wouldn't get too cranky about the wedding plans.

"It means the sky's the limit." Lori threw her hands in the air. "We'll do anything to ensure your wedding is unforgettable. Have you picked out your wedding attire yet?" She asked, then shoved a truffle in her mouth.

"Carter, didn't you mention something about Dior?" Asher asked, surprising me. I couldn't believe he remembered. "At Saks Fifth Avenue?"

"Yes, but I want to hear all of our options before deciding." I grinned at Lori.

"Dior makes incredible clothes, but before you order the suits, I want you to entertain the idea of having your suits custom made by a local designer. Her name is, um, it's on the tip of my tongue." Lori patted the side of her nose with a pen.

"Oh yes, Mitzi Evans. She graduated from VCU three years ago, and has made quite a name for herself designing bridal gowns."

"Well, neither of us is wearing a gown, but we'll keep an open mind about her." The urge to laugh hit me, but I stifled it. "Do you have examples of her work with menswear?"

"Of course." Lori opened her briefcase, pulled out a tablet, and promptly dropped it. "I feel strange." She mumbled, then picked it up and started tapping. A moment later, she tried to hand it to me, but Mom grabbed it instead.

"Ooh, this is handsome." Mom said, and Asher and I both leaned in to see. "Though maybe you should go with a gown, Carter."

"Pardon me?"

Mom flushed. "Honey, I didn't mean to say that. It's just I can't stop thinking about you in a white wedding gown. It would be so funny."

Asher looked around Mom at me, shaking his head with wide-open eyes. Then he tilted his head toward the half-eaten tray of chocolates.

Oh shit. They were laced.

Mary Jane bit her lower lip, and Granny's eyes took on a pink sheen.

"May I speak with you for a moment, Mary Jane?" I stood, and she blinked. "In private."

I stalked into the kitchen. Florida was arranging finger foods on a platter. When Mary Jane crept in, I pointed at the tray of meats and cheeses. "Since everyone is about to get the munchies, I guess we'll need all the food we can get." I put my face in my hands and sighed. "Poor Mom. Why did you serve us edibles? Jesus, my mother has never done drugs before in her life, and now she wants me in drag for the fucking wedding!" My voice rose with each word.

Florida eyed Mary Jane. "You didn't."

"I'm sorry, it was an accident. Last night I made some for myself, and some for everybody else." She shrugged. "I must have picked up the wrong tray." Her voice quivered with remorse. "Please, forgive me."

Thudding beats came from the living room, and I heard feet racing down the hallway.

"Carter, your mother, she's losing it." Asher's face was stark white. "She turned on the stereo, and her and Granny are arguing over whether I should wear the wedding gown, or you."

"Oh dear." Mary Jane reminded me of the maid Esmerelda from the old tv show Bewitched. You could tell she wanted to fade away into nothing.

Florida grabbed Mary Jane by the shoulders. "Jesus Christ, woman. What the hell have you done?"

"Oh dear!"

I opened my mouth to speak, but nothing came out. My shoulders sagged. Then Asher wrapped me in his arms and kissed my forehead. "Baby, it's going to be alright. Just don't tell your mother. She'll think it's the wine. I'm sure Mary Jane didn't mean to do it, right?"

Mary Jane wailed pathetically, wringing her hands, then the three of us walked out of the kitchen in single file. When we got back to the living room, I almost fainted in disbelief.

"Sissy, you should come over more often." Granny was saying to Mom. They were seated next to each other, apparently having quite the conversation. Lila Brooke snatched a truffle off the tray and stuffed it in her mouth. Her foot was tapping to the 60s rock music. Lori Stallings, on the other hand, was not handling things very well.

She was seated on the floor, an open makeup compact in

hand. When she glanced up at us, an odd grin spread across her face.

"Are you okay, Lori?" Asher bent over to help her, but she just laughed.

"I've fallen, and I can't get up."

CHAPTER 26

ASHER

"Let me help you up." I reached a hand down to Lori. She grabbed it, but instead of getting to her feet, she pulled me down to the floor. I landed on my ass next to her. "Ouch!"

"Are you sure you're gay?" The woman winked and licked her lips. "Because if I had my way, I'd lick you from your head to your toes."

Carter cleared his throat, then reached down and pulled me to my feet. "Miss Stallings, trust me, Asher is extra gay. And if you flirt with him again, we'll give you a demonstration to prove it." He dragged me away from her.

"I'm not sure hiring her is a good idea." I muttered. "She's very unprofessional."

"Lori is very stoned, and probably won't remember any of this." Carter whispered. "What are we going to do when she sobers up? Mary Jane drugged her. She could sue us, or worse."

"Oh, shit." I giggled. The one piece of chocolate I'd eaten was kicking in, and I wanted more. I strolled over to the coffee table and reached down for another piece, but Carter stopped me.

"You're a lawyer. We've got to keep our wits about us, and figure out what the hell we're going to tell Lori." Carter whispered, combing his hair back with his fingers. "Though another piece of chocolate might make things..." Florida swooped into the living room. "What are you doing?"

Florida snagged the tray off the table. "If you keep eating Satan's candy, you're going to screw things up worse than they already are." She hissed and raced back to the kitchen.

"Damn." Carter muttered, then we both slowly spun around, taking in the scenery. Sissy and Granny were laughing it up on the couch. Lila Brooke was fiddling with the stereo, and Mary Jane was nibbling on a piece of chocolate, a serene smile splitting her face. Lori Stallings had managed to get back in the chair and was attempting to apply lipstick. Bless her heart, but she couldn't keep the bright red shade inside the lip lines. "She looks like a clown." Carter snickered, and I giggled along with him.

"So, what the hell are we doing now?" I asked, then took Carter's arm and steered him into the study and shut the door behind us. "You're right, this is a lawsuit waiting to happen. How can we fix it?"

Carter sank into a leather armchair and laughed. "The only way to fix it is to get them drunk. Then we can blame it on the booze. Jesus, we're all going to need rehab after tonight."

I squeezed in next to him and laid my head on his shoulder. "I'm so dizzy," I giggled. "Damn, Mary Jane must have put extra weed in that chocolate. I haven't been this high since college."

"We still need to work on the wedding." Carter sighed. "Though I have to admit, it's starting to be more trouble than it's worth. But, we would definitely make a statement by

marrying at CCV. The first same-sex wedding ever held there."
He kissed my cheek, and I snuggled in closer. "I love you so
much, Asher. Can we just hide in here until the lunatics sober
up and go home?"

"It's tempting." I reluctantly sat up straight and looked
Carter in the eye. "We have to go back in there and get them
drunk. Or at least give them enough booze so the wedding
planner doesn't realize it was the chocolates." I stood up and
pulled Carter to his feet. "Come on, let's get Florida. She knows
how to wrangle stoners and drunks better than any person on
the planet."

―――――

"They're already messed up." Florida put her hands on her
hips and glared at us. "Why would you want them to be drunk,
too?"

Carter snickered, and I couldn't look him in the eye. If I did,
I'd collapse into a ball of hysterical laughter. "It's because of
that woman. What's her name again?"

"Lori Stallings." Carter giggled. "If she finds out she was
doped, she could take us to court. Hell, we could all be arrest-
ed." Carter barked, then held his sides to contain his laughter.

"Boy, that's not funny." Florida rolled up a dish towel and
snapped Carter in the arm with it. "What the hell was Mary
Jane thinking?"

"She made a mistake, that's all." I took the towel from Florida, then spied the tray of chocolates on the counter behind her.
It was tempting to eat another one, but not until we'd taken
care of this mess. "Mary Jane said she brought the wrong batch
of chocolates. The unlaced truffles are at her and Lila Brooke's
house."

"Can you whip up a punch real quick?" Carter asked. "You

know, something high octane. Oh! Margarita's would be perfect. Then we can blame the mess on tequila."

"Excellent idea." I crossed the room to the pantry.

"Tequila ain't in there." Florida said, then she opened the freezer and pulled out a bottle. "But the mixers are. Bring me a punch bowl too, Asher."

I found what she wanted and placed them on the granite island.

"Make it extra strong." Carter waggled his eyebrows. "The girls won't know what hit them."

———

When Carter and I strolled back to the living room, we froze in the doorway. Granny and Sissy were flipping through the fabric samples Lori brought, acting like the best of friends. Lila Brooke was staring deep into Mary Jane's eyes, and I wondered if I should send them upstairs to one of the guest rooms. Our wedding planner was engrossed with whatever was on her tablet. It definitely wasn't a makeup tutorial, since one of her painted-on eyebrows was smeared.

We strolled in, then Carter clapped his hands to get the ladies' attention.

"I hope you're having a wonderful time." He bared his teeth. "Before we begin the wedding stuff, I want to propose a toast."

Florida pushed a cart into the living room laden with a punch bowl and margarita glasses. She poured everyone a drink and passed them around.

"To my soon-to-be husband, Asher." He threw his arm around me, and I almost fell down. "I love you more than, um, well, anything on the planet."

"To Asher!" Everyone called out, and they all drained their drinks.

"Florida, would you mind refilling everyone's cocktail?" I asked her, and she went around the room filling everyone's cups.

"I feel funny." Lori mumbled. "Maybe I shouldn't have anymore." Florida snatched the glass from her and filled it.

"Drink it." Florida glared at the woman and handed her a full glass. "If you know what's good for ya."

Lori blinked, and her tablet clattered to the floor.

"Oh my stars!" Granny pointed at the tablet. Sissy gasped, and I picked it up to see what the problem was.

"Ooh, Carter." I showed him the tablet, and he fell down on the sofa clutching his sides, laughing. Two naked men were in the middle of, well, doing things naked men do with each other.

"Give me that back!" Lori reached for it, and I let her have it. "I just wanted to see what you gay guys actually do in bed. You know, because I'm marrying you two."

"Huh?" I tilted my head in her direction.

"So, which one of you is the man, and which one of you is the woman?" She giggled, then turned the tablet on its side and gazed at it with an odd look on her face.

"Neither." Lila Brooke called out. "It's two men, sweetie."

"Oh." Lori's left eyebrow rose, which looked odd since her right brow was nearly gone. "Are all gay guys this um, well endowed?" She turned the tablet so everyone could see it. Sissy and Granny had the vapors. "Like, I've never been with a man who was, well, you know, so big."

I winked at Carter, who winked back. "Carter is."

Every woman gasped, all eyes glued to him. He smacked my ass and guffawed. "Don't tell them that!"

"Well, you are." I fell back on the couch next to him, and he nuzzled my neck.

"Lucky." Lori slurred, then drained her drink.

Florida grabbed her glass and refilled it. "Drink it."

Lori's bloodshot eyes widened, then she took the glass and sipped. I noticed the punchbowl was getting low.

"Carter, let's go to the kitchen and make some more." I grabbed his hand, and we almost fell over when we stood up. We stumbled toward the kitchen, and when we got there, a strange girl was standing in the doorway.

"Who are you?" I asked, my voice slurring.

"I found her sitting on the front step." Mom's voice called out. She must have come home early from her date. "What was your name again, child?"

"Mindy." The girl stepped aside so we could enter the kitchen. "Miss Stalling's assistant."

"Oh, we forgot about you." Carter grinned.

I saw a small brown stain on her upper lip, and leaned in for a closer look. "Oh shit." I pointed at her mouth. "Is that chocolate?"

"Yes, dear." Mom called out, and Carter and I raced into the kitchen. "I found a tray of truffles, and Thom and I couldn't resist. We gave her one too."

My heart stopped for a moment, and Carter clutched his chest. "You, um, ate the chocolates?"

"They're delicious!" Judge Gottwald grinned, and mother eyed me suspiciously. "My compliments to the chef. Who made them?"

Shit. We'd drugged a judge. If ever we were to go to prison, it would probably be now.

"Mom." My voice was shaking. "Can we speak with you? Alone?"

CHAPTER 27

ASHER

Mom plastered a smile on her face. "Of course, darling. It's about the wedding, right?" She winked at us, then without another word, Mom led us out of the kitchen. When she got to the living room, she halted in the doorway and muttered, "What on earth?"

"You got that right." I sighed. Lori Stallings was still staring at her tablet, most likely watching gay porn. Granny, Sissy, Lila Brook, and Mary Jane were dancing around the living room to an old Donna Summer song.

Mom gave a little wave at the ladies, who all ignored us. She then led us into the study and shut the door behind us. Mom sat behind the desk, drumming her fingers on the wood. "Normally I enjoy a party, boys, but I'm not sure if Thom is prepared for our special version of fun."

"Mom." I combed my hair back with my fingers and sighed. "It's worse than that."

"Mary Jane made the chocolates." Carter leaned against the wall, staring at Mom. She shrugged, then reality settled on her shoulders.

"Please, for the love of all things holy, tell me they're just plain chocolates, and not the fun kind?" She clutched the strand of pearls around her neck.

A giggle bubbled up my throat.

"Please, don't tell me I fed Thom Gottwald, a federal judge, laced baked goods." Mom groaned. "Fuck."

Carter's eyes widened. Mom rarely cursed.

"Well, you fed them to both Thom and Mindy, to be accurate." I giggled again. There was absolutely nothing funny about this, but I couldn't stop myself. "She didn't do it on purpose. Mary Jane says she made two batches, one with weed, and the other without. She just brought the wrong ones."

"It doesn't matter." Mom's fingers tightened around the pearls. "How am I going to explain to Thom, a man I'm happily dating, that I fed him marijuana?"

"Well, my mother is tripping on drugs for the first time in her life, and we also doped the event coordinator for CCV." Carter put his face in his hands and sighed. "So, what we've done to fix it is get them hammered with margaritas. That way, we can blame it on tequila."

"And of course, Thom isn't much of a drinker, and that young girl I found on the front steps doesn't even look old enough to drink." Mom slammed the top of the desk with the hand not clutching the pearls. "Do you know how many laws we're breaking? How much money we could lose if this were to become a civil case?"

"Haha haha!" I couldn't stop myself.

Mom's lips twisted, and I noticed her eyes were definitely pink.

"Marjorie, I don't know what else we can do." Carter squeezed in the leather wingback chair next to me. "We have to get them drunk. And why are you dating someone who doesn't drink?"

"I um, I don't know." Mom stood up, and I noticed her sway just a bit. Mom never ate Mary Jane's edibles. "Well, we have no other option. We've got to get Thom drunk, and I guess that young girl too. Shit. Shit. Shit."

We got out of the chair, and I fell to my knees. "Ouch!" Carter helped me up, nearly falling over himself. When I opened the door leading to the living room, there wasn't anyone there. They'd also cut the music. "Where the hell did they go?"

"They went downstairs to the theater." Florida entered the room pushing a cart with a full punchbowl of margaritas on it. Suddenly, you could hear and feel beats coming from the floor. "Said something about karaoke."

"Where's the judge and that young woman, Florida?" Mom asked.

"They went downstairs, too." Florida shook her head dramatically. "Mary Jane deserves to be horsewhipped."

"Florida, she's in her 70s, and her memory isn't what it used to be." Mom strolled into the hallway outside the living room, where we had a small elevator. We followed along, and when the doors slid open, Mom gestured for Florida to go first. It was installed after my father fell ill and couldn't take the steps anymore. We all squeezed in, and when the elevator began its descent, Carter and I grabbed each other.

"Oh my God, I felt like I was going to fall over." Mom giggled. "Jesus, I hate being stoned."

Florida crossed her arms over her chest and scowled at all of us. "The good lord didn't intend people to smoke that stuff."

"We smoked nothing." Mom huffed, and a goofy smile spread across her cheeks. "I hope Thom is okay."

When the doors slid open, loud guitars and an off-key female voice screeched at us. The music grew in volume as we walked through the basement. When we got to the small theater, I opened the door and cringed.

"What an awful song." I said "Why does Lila Brooke always have to sing Iron Butterfly?"

"It's tragic." Carter shook his head.

"It was popular when they were young." Mom said, and Florida pushed the cart into the room with us on her heels.

Lila Brooke was on the tiny stage in front of the movie screen, screaming into the orange microphone. "In a gadda da vida, baby! Don't you know..." The song abruptly ended, and Lila Brooke almost fell over. "Hey, who cut the sound?"

"It's my turn." Granny stumbled onto the stage and took the mike from her. While the two of them argued about whose turn it was, we saw the judge trying to make conversation with Lori Stallings. Her assistant was sitting on the floor rocking back and forth, her glazed eyes like saucers.

"Oh shit." I pointed at her, and Florida swooped in and passed her a cup of booze. "I can't believe we're serving a potentially underage girl liquor in front of a judge."

Mom grabbed a margarita and hurried over to Judge Gottwald. At first he tried to say no to the drink, but Mom was a very determined woman. He finally took the glass and drained half of it at once. Mom discreetly winked in our direction.

"I'm not sure how much more of this I can take." Carter said, and his arm went around my waist. "You know, I used to like these wild parties your family throws, but this is too much."

Sissy finally noticed us and strolled over. She'd kicked her shoes off somewhere, and her eyes were half-shut. "You were right, Carter. The Yates are so much fun! I just needed to relax."

I snickered, and Carter bit his lip.

"Sissy!" Granny's voice roared through the hidden speakers.

"Get up on this fucking stage with me. I'll be Kiki Dee and you sing Elton John's part." Mom's eyes lit up, and she stumbled up to the stage. A few seconds later, they were destroying the song 'Don't Go Breaking My Heart.'

"Looks like Granny made a new friend." I drawled, and Carter rolled his eyes. "Hey, I think it's a good thing. Your mother always felt left out, and now she's having the time of her life."

"I wonder how she'd feel about it if she knew the truth." Carter sighed. "That the reason for her sudden acceptance is entirely because of Mary Jane accidentally drugging everybody. Oh, and I think the chocolate is finally wearing off." Carter yawned.

"Yeah, I'm coming down too." I said, then Carter pulled me in closer. "Oh wow." I pointed at my Mom, who was making out with Judge Gottwald. "I've never seen Mom kiss anyone but my father. This feels very weird."

"Well, at least the man's been drinking. Now we don't need to worry that he'll find out the truth." Carter said, then he pointed at the young girl, Mindy. She'd gotten to her feet and was drifting toward the stage. When she got there, Mindy tilted her head, and started singing along to the lyrics scrolling on the tiny television monitor. "And it looks like she's cutting loose, too."

Lori Stallings stumbled over to the girl. Then she put her arm around her waist and joined her in a sing-a-long. Apparently, everyone loved Elton John and Kiki Dee. Granny and Sissy were tripping all over the stage, acting out the lyrics. Florida stood in a corner, grimly surveying the party.

"Asher." Carter spoke into my ear.

"Yes."

"Nobody's looking. Do you want to get out of here?" He kissed me below my ear, and my legs felt like spaghetti. Since I was exhausted by the evening's shenanigans, his suggestion was perfect. I grabbed Carter's hand, and we both turned toward the door.

"Let's go."

———

Nobody noticed our exit. Since neither of us had much to drink, our buzz was rapidly fading. But, I was glad. I knew Carter loved all the parties my family threw. For me they'd become boring and repetitive. All I wanted was to curl up next to Carter and spend the night in his arms.

"Look up." Carter pointed at the night sky. "Make a wish."

A shooting star shot across the heavens. I knew what I wanted, but doubted my wish would come true. Carter brushed his lips across mine and sighed.

"What did you wish for?" I asked, then I let go of him, opened the door to Carter's Mercedes and slid into the front seat.

Once Carter was behind the wheel, he turned to me and frowned. "I feel stupid."

"Why?"

"Because of my wish." His brow furrowed. "For the longest time, I've wanted a massive wedding. Something so over the top that no one would ever forget it."

My mouth went dry. Would my wish come true after all?

He switched on the ignition and we slowly drove toward our cottage. "And?" I prompted him to continue.

"Honestly, all I want is to be married to you without all the fuss." He glanced back at the house. "And I want no more of that craziness. It's exhausting."

"That's why I married you on that mountain, Carter. So we wouldn't have to deal with the lunatics I'm related to." I said.

"And even though I'll do whatever you want regarding our marriage, if I had my way, we'd fly away somewhere quiet. Just the two of us, and I'd marry you again."

Carter stomped on the brakes, and I nearly flew out of the seat.

"Let's do it then." Carter's eyes blazed.

"Do what?" I asked, praying he'd say what I desperately wanted.

"Elope."

CHAPTER 28

CARTER

"Yes!" Asher smacked his palms together. "When do you want to do it?"

"Considering the events of the last few hours, I say let's do it now." I began driving again, and a moment later, our cottage came into view. "When we get inside, pack an overnight bag. Oh yeah, we need to figure out where we're going."

"Vegas?" Asher asked.

"It's so tacky there." I parked the car, and we both raced to the door. "Colorado again?"

Asher snorted, then slid his key in the lock. "I'd rather us go somewhere with competent officials. Why risk another wedding setback?"

The door opened, and we raced inside. "Asher, pack for both of us while I pull out my laptop and figure out the best place for us to go."

Asher grasped my forearms and drew me in close. "I love you so damn much." He murmured, and when his lips brushed across mine, our noses bumped. My heart felt so massive whenever he touched me. I smacked his ass, and Asher let go of me and raced up the stairs.

I couldn't remember where I'd put the laptop, then I recalled using it last in Asher's home office. While walking past the stairs, I heard Asher whistling a tune. "It's been a while since I've heard him this happy." I sighed, and dizziness shimmered through me. Wherever we went, it was best if we weren't driving. Most of the effects of the laced chocolates were gone, but it made little sense to risk getting into an accident.

I found the laptop and typed best states quick marriage into the search engine. "Huh. Washington D.C. is the closest. We can hire a driver, speed up there, and we'll be married tomorrow." I glanced through the other choices. "I've never been to Oregon, or Idaho."

For the life of me, I couldn't figure out what had changed my mind about having a big ceremony at CCV. On paper, it was the logical choice. I loved big events and parties. But the thought of dealing with the asylum up the driveway made my skin crawl. I loved them all dearly, but I had to admit that tonight's party had sapped whatever will I had to keep them all in line. Plus, this wasn't my first time at the rodeo.

"This crazy stuff happens with alarming regularity up there." I muttered, and when I glanced up, I saw Asher in the doorway. He'd packed us each an overnight bag, and his eyes glittered with excitement.

"Yes, now you see why I wanted to avoid a big wedding." Asher placed the bags on the floor and sat across from me. "But, before we elope, make sure it's the right decision for you, Carter. I'm happy marrying you in a quickie ceremony, or at the country club. Whatever makes you happy. I just don't want you to regret it years from now." His blue eyes locked on mine.

"Let's get out of here. I didn't know this, but Washington D.C. is an excellent city for getting a fast and easy ceremony. We could wait until morning to hit the road, or we could..." I began, but Asher held up his hand.

"If we wait around, everyone will find out, and they'll try to stop us." Asher came around to my side of the desk and perched on the edge. "Let's go tonight. It's only..." Asher pulled his phone out of his pocket, "...eight o'clock." He typed on his phone, then grinned at me. "The last train for D.C. leaves at ten. We'll wake up tomorrow morning and get married before anyone can stop us."

"Call an Uber." I stood and kissed Asher on the cheek. "I can't wait for our honeymoon."

———

"Did you remember to tell the driver to keep driving past the main house?"

We were standing outside on our front porch, both of us checking the time every few seconds. It felt like we'd been waiting here forever, and we had to make it to the train station in a matter of minutes.

"Yes, of course." Asher huffed, tapping his foot impatiently. It was an eerie night, with wisps of fog blowing around the grounds. A female voice yelled in the distance.

"What the hell was that?" My hand flew to my chest.

"Who cares?" Asher pointed up the driveway. "The driver's here." Headlights were slowly heading toward us, and a few moments later, we were piling into the back seat of a red Nissan sedan.

"The train station on Staples Mill Road, right?" The driver asked. He was a little younger than both of us and had bright red hair with skin covered in freckles.

"Yes, and step on it. Our train leaves at ten." Asher shut the door, and the driver turned the car around and began driving toward River Road. We passed the main house without incident, then with a stifled scream, the driver slammed on the brakes.

"What the hell is that?" He pointed toward his passenger window.

"Jesus." I muttered. Like a scene out of a zombie movie, a tall blonde woman covered in dirt and leaves was stumbling toward the car. "It's Lori Stallings. Oh, and that girl is right behind her. Driver, please hurry. We have to get away from them!"

We didn't have to tell him twice. The tires squealed as we raced past the wedding planner and her messed-up assistant. I heard another scream, and both Asher and I turned in our seats to see what it was.

"Aw, bless her heart." Lori had fallen down, and while we watched, the girl Mindy tripped over her. I pointed at them. "Asher, that is why we're eloping."

––––––––

"Good morning." I stretched my legs out, then laid my head on Asher's chest.

"Good morning." Asher's voice rumbled in my ear. "But it's only morning for about twenty more minutes. We need to hurry and get our marriage license."

I barely remembered checking into The Four Seasons last night. Even though we'd both slept for the two-hour train ride, I still felt exhausted. But it was tinged with excitement. Finally, after enduring one catastrophe after another, we were getting married in peace.

"Have you checked your phone?" I asked, because I was afraid of checking mine.

"No." Asher replied. "But I guess we have to let them know

we're alive. Here." Asher sat up and handed me my phone from off the nightstand. Then he grabbed his phone and started scrolling. "How bizarre." He showed me the screen and said, "I only have one message from Mom."

> Don't blame you one bit

I snickered, then saw there were zero messages on mine. "They're all recovering from the party last night and think we're back at the cottage."

"Mom probably didn't drink too much because of the judge." Asher shook his head. "I imagine she sent Florida to the cottage to find us this morning, and when we weren't there, she put two and two together."

Asher tapped on the screen, then showed me the message he'd sent.

> Let everyone know we're alive and we've eloped

———

"Sign here and here." The woman behind the glass screen passed our marriage license through the tiny metal opening at the bottom. "That will be $45, please."

Asher handed her a credit card, and I pulled a pen out of my jacket pocket and scrawled my name. Then Asher wrote his name, and a minute later, she handed him a receipt.

"The justice of the peace is on the third floor." The woman grinned. "Congratulations."

"Thanks." We spun around and raced for the elevator. It was already after three, and the courthouse closed at 4:30. We didn't want to come back in the morning, and had already decided to fly to Colorado and spend a quiet week there for our honeymoon.

The elevator doors slid open, and there was no one else on it. When the doors shut, I heard Asher's phone buzzing. "God, I hope it's not family." He fished it out of his pocket, and a moment later it clattered to the floor.

"Oh shit."

I picked it up and read the message. It was from Marjorie.

> Lori Stallings is threatening to sue for breach of contract

"How can she sue when we didn't sign anything?" I asked, and for a moment I worried we had signed something while we were stoned last night. Asher took the phone back, and a smile spread across his cheeks.

"She can't. But," he took a deep breath. "The good news is she's not threatening us with a lawsuit over that stupid party last night."

The elevator opened on the third floor in front of the courtroom we were going to. "Let's hope there isn't a line."

Asher held the door to the courtroom open for me. There was only one couple ahead of us, taking their vows before the judge. We sat down and waited for our turn. The couple being married was a middle-aged man and woman, and they had huge smiles plastered on their faces.

My phone buzzed, and when I pulled it out, I saw a message from Mom.

> You eloped

> I wanted to see you get married

"Hey, do you think they'd let us record our wedding?" I whispered to Asher.

"Is that your mother?"

"Yes."

"I doubt the judge will have a problem with it. It's not like this is a sensitive court case." Asher pointed at a man in a police uniform. "That's the bailiff. When it's our turn, I'll ask him to hold the phone so Sissy can see it live."

> Mom you will see it
>
> Turn on FaceTime
>
> We're in a courtroom so don't make a sound

A moment later, Mom's face filled the screen, and I saw Asher's grandmother too. I nudged Asher, and we both waved at the screen. Granny opened her mouth to say something, but Mom hushed her.

"Next." The judge's voice boomed, and my heart rate skyrocketed. Asher and I stood, then walked toward the bench. Asher handed the bailiff the paperwork, and the judge looked it over.

"Everything's as it should be." The judge signed the papers and grinned at us. She was an older woman with what had to be a black wig on.

"Your honor, is it okay for the bailiff to hold a phone so our families who couldn't be here today can see us being married?" Asher asked, and I held up the phone so Mom and Granny could see what was happening.

"What a lovely idea." She smiled, then I handed the phone to the grinning bailiff. "This happens all the time."

The bailiff glanced down at the screen and snickered. Then he held the phone so we could see the screen, and Granny was holding a champagne flute up to us.

"Are we ready to begin the ceremony?" The judge asked,

and despite cold sweat running down my sides, I nodded. This was a dream come true, to be married twice to this wonderful man I loved more than life itself. Asher took my hand in his, and he turned to me and I saw a solitary tear slide down his cheek.

"The step that each of you are about to undergo is one of the most important events in life that any two people can undertake. It is the entering into a union, a union between two men founded upon mutual respect and affection. Because of this unique relationship that you both are voluntarily partaking in, your individual lives will change, and, resulting from this change, your responsibilities will intensify significantly, but your joy will also intensify significantly if you are sincere with your pledge that you are about to make to one another today." The judge said, then she proceeded with the rest of the ceremony.

"Asher Bartholomew Yates, will you take Carter Camden as your husband, to love and comfort him through life's ups and downs, and forsaking all others?"

Another tear escaped his eyes, and he whispered, "Yes, I will."

"Carter Camden, will you take Asher Bartholomew Yates as your husband, to love and comfort him through all of life's ups and downs, and forsaking all others?"

I opened my mouth, and a sob tore through me. "Yes, oh yes, I will."

"That's my baby boy!" I heard Mom's voice through the phone, and the judge laughed.

"Gentlemen, take each other's hands, please." The judge commanded, and now we were facing each other. Asher reached over and wiped a tear off my cheek with his thumb. "Repeat after me, Mr. Yates. I, Asher Bartholomew Yates, take Carter Camden to be my wedded husband, to have and to hold, for better for worse, for richer for poorer, to love and to cherish, from this day forward."

Asher's voice trembled as he spoke the vows. I heard faint sobbing and realized it was Mom and Granny. After I spoke my vows, the judge continued.

"Do you have rings?" She asked, and I realized I still had my old one on, and so did Asher.

"Do you want us to remove these and put them back on? We were married once before and…" I rambled, and the judge held up her hand.

"No, leave them on. It's the words that matter most." She said. "Let these rings be given and received as a token of your affection, sincerity, and fidelity to one another. Now repeat after me, Mr. Camden. With this ring, I thee wed."

"With this ring I thee wed." My voice was barely a whisper. Asher repeated the words, too.

"In as much as Carter Camden and Asher Bartholomew Yates have consented together in wedlock and have witnessed the same before this company and pledged their vows to each other, by the authority vested in me by the District of Columbia, I now pronounce the two of you married." The judge sighed, and I heard more crying come from the phone. "Please kiss each other, or your family is going to lose it." She laughed.

"I love you so much, Carter." Asher's blue eyes were wet, and a moment later his lips crashed into mine. I wrapped my arms around Asher, and when the kiss broke, I whispered in his ear. "I love you more than anything I've ever known, and more than I'll ever love anyone else."

EPILOGUE

ASHER- ONE YEAR LATER

"r. Yates, your mother wants to speak to you." My secretary's voice rang through the intercom.

"Send her in."

A moment later, Mom strolled into my office, laying her briefcase on the edge of my desk. "Hello, darling." She went to the mini-bar and fixed herself a cocktail. "Have you finished the Clemson deal? Because their merger with Manchester Iron-works is giving my client Joe Barclay a massive headache." She settled in the chair in front of my desk.

"Yes, Mom. I signed the contracts yesterday afternoon." I said, wondering why she was here. Mom knew the deal was done already, so she was probably using that as a pretense for something else.

"I know we're saving money in this smaller office space, but I miss my old office. It had so much more room." Mom sipped her drink, and I noticed she wouldn't meet my gaze. There was something amiss. "Darling, I need to tell you something, and I need you to remain calm."

Since I was the calmest member of the family, this had to be huge. "Sure. What is it?"

"Judge Gottwald has asked for my hand in marriage." She finally met my gaze. "I've agreed."

"Oh." That was unexpected. Mom and the judge had been dating for a year now, and while I knew they got along, I never realized how serious it had become. "Congratulations."

"Thank you, but there are several practical matters that must be addressed first." Mom stood and began pacing around the office. "First, I hoped that Thom and I could live in your cottage. He doesn't want to live in the home he shared with Elizabeth," Mom was referring to Thom's dead wife. "And I don't want to live in the same home I shared with your father. Plus, Mother frightens him."

I snickered, and Mom winked.

"If you are agreeable, we'll pay you and Carter rent." Mom drained her drink, then walked over to the bar and pulled out a bottle of water. Ever since she and the judge started dating, her alcohol consumption had dropped considerably.

"You don't have to pay us rent, Mom. It's on your land." I grinned.

"There's another thing. I was going to take you out to dinner to discuss this, but we might as well get it over with." She sat again and twisted the bottle open. "I want to retire."

"What?"

"Not completely, because I love the law. What I'm proposing is that I handle the firm's pro bono work." This was free work our associates performed for the community. "As it stands, each attorney just does the minimum one hundred forty hours a year. I want to organize it better, so that our legal talents actually do good work. And it's time for me to step down and allow you to shine as the managing partner."

"Wow, I don't know what to say. Do you think I'm ready?" I

held a hand up, then buzzed Gloria. "Please, hold all calls and visitors for the next hour. Thank you."

"You are as ready as I was when I took over. Plus, it's not like I'm going anywhere. I'll still keep my office here, it's just that my focus will now be on working with the community. I want us to be more involved with specific charities, ones that struggle to get decent legal representation. Plus, we can…"

As Mom told me her plans for the future, I thought of mine, too. Being the managing partner of the most successful law firm in the state was a massive career milestone. And now that Carter and the architects were busy designing our future home in Manakin-Sabot, I had a little more leeway with time.

"Darling, are you listening to me?" Mom waved her hand in front of my face.

"Of course, Mom. And whatever your future holds, be assured that Carter and I will support you."

———

"Thanks, Charles." I tossed the keys to the Jaguar to our doorman, who parked it in the lot for me. He was an old man, almost as old as The Tuckahoe, which was built in 1927.

After Carter and I eloped, we decided that living so close to family wasn't healthy for our relationship. Carter was insistent that he design the perfect house, and since it would take a year or two to design and build it, we moved out of the cottage. We bought a small condo at The Tuckahoe as a temporary home, and we'd rent it out after we moved into our new one. It was a lovely building and was on the list of National Historic buildings. But, it was far too small for Carter. Hell, he'd been forced to put most of his wardrobe in storage. As for me, I didn't care where we lived as long as I woke up next to Carter every morning.

I got on the elevator and pushed the number for our floor, grateful to be the only one in the small space. The ladies who drank weren't thrilled when we moved out, and neither was Florida. But the most important of the ladies, Mom and Sissy, were very supportive. Both understood that it was time for us to be on our own, and since The Tuckahoe was a ten minute drive down River Road, we popped in at least once per week, usually for one of their parties.

The elevator door opened, and I sauntered to the end of the hallway and opened our front door. "What's that smell?" I sniffed the air. It smelled like something was baking in the oven. Since neither of us enjoyed cooking much, that meant we had visitors.

Sissy's head popped through the kitchen doorway. "Hi, Asher. I hope you don't mind, but Mary Jane is teaching me how to bake."

"You mean she's teaching you how to get baked with baked goods, right?" I grinned, and Sissy laughed. Ever since that wild night at Mom's house, Sissy had become a mild stoner. Not as bad as the rest of the family, but she enjoyed the occasional brownie. "Where's Carter?"

"In the study. He found a design flaw in the plans for the house, so he's trying to fix them before the contractors begin construction." Sissy replied, and I hurried down the hallway to make sure he wasn't flipping out.

Over the last year, he'd grown calmer, and was less prone to temper tantrums. We'd gone to a few counseling sessions with Belinda Therapista, but after moving away from Mom's house, we discovered we didn't need her help.

The door to the study was open, and when I walked in, Carter stood and gave me a bone-crushing hug.

"The architect messed up the kitchen plans, so I'm fixing it." Carter pecked my cheek. "How was your day?"

I sat in the chair in front of the desk and put my feet up on the edge. "Mom is getting married to Thom, and wants to live in the cottage with him." I chuckled. "Thom is a little afraid of Granny."

Carter shrugged his shoulders and smiled. "I don't blame him one bit."

"And, drum roll please," I imitated one on my knees. "Mom is retiring and I'm becoming the managing partner of the firm. This will take a few months since her caseload needs to wind down, but she's going to take over our charitable work."

"That's wonderful news." Carter said. "Is that what you want, or are you just going along with it?"

"Well, it means more work, but the law runs in the blood. I love the firm, though not as much as I love you." I bit my lower lip, and Carter got up, came around the desk, and kissed the top of my head.

"I have everything I want, well, except a large enough closet. But that's being taken care of soon." Carter said, and I took my feet off the desk and Carter sat on my lap. "And I love you more than you'll ever know, Asher."

"Not as much as I love you." I brushed my lips over his, then we both heard footsteps approaching from the hallway.

"I made some chocolates with Sissy." Mary Jane grinned. "They're excellent. Want to try one?"

Carter's eyes locked with mine, and he smirked.

"No, thanks, Mary Jane."

———

The story of Asher and Carter was a hoot to write, and I hope you enjoyed reading it as much as I did writing it. Here is a sample chapter of the first book in the Southern Discomfort series The Cad & Dad for you to enjoy.

"I'm going into town for a few hours. Are you going to be okay by yourself?"

"Yes, I've got plenty to keep myself busy." Cary pointed at his laptop, then gestured toward the papers covering the bed. Every day his assistant sent more of his work here, which worried me. Like, would he ever leave my house?

"Text me if you need anything."

I turned to go and he spoke. "Where are you going?"

"Well, if you must know, I've an appointment with my therapist." Why I felt compelled to tell him the truth baffled me. I should have said anything but that. Cary's eyes widened, and a slow smile spread across his cheeks.

"I've already told you that you don't need a shrink. You're as sane and steady as they come, Thatch." Cary said, and I noticed something different in his eyes. If I wasn't mistaken, he actually cared about me, or at the very least he was an excellent actor.

"Thank you, Cary. But every once in a while it's good for me to check in with her. She gives me a different perspective on things, and right now I could use that." I said, then turned to leave, but Cary spoke again.

"If you ever want to talk, I'm all ears."

———

I'd first gone to see Cris Foster when Brian filed for divorce. She'd had a calming effect on me, and helped me realize that I was in charge of my emotional well-being, not my ex-husband. Before I started therapy, I thought seeing a therapist was a waste of time. What kept me going back to her was silly, but I was glad I stuck it out. Her name was the same as my favorite character on The Young And The Restless, a soap opera my granny and I watched together when I was a kid. It was a stupid reason, but watching the stories, as my granny called them, was the beginning of my love affair with telling stories of my own.

Blue Ridge Pride Behavioral Associates was in a plain, one-story brick house on the other side of Asheville. There were only three therapists and a receptionist. A trans friend who found their help invaluable had referred me to them as he was transitioning. After three years of weekly visits I announced that I felt healed enough to stop coming. Now I was back with my tail between my legs.

As I stepped out of my SUV onto the gravel driveway, the front door opened and a woman stepped out, tears streaming down her face. My first instinct was to comfort her, but when she saw me she covered her face with her hand and ran to her car.

"God, am I so confused about my life that I want to reopen old wounds?" I muttered, then forced myself to move.

Suddenly, I remembered being that woman. Reliving every drama Brian and I had gone through. But, it was worth it in the end. We might have been divorced, but Brian and I kept our friendship and business arrangements going, thanks to Cris.

"Thatch, it's good to see you again!" The receptionist said when I walked through the door. His name was Tim, and he also taught yoga and reiki at the new age bookstore downtown.

"Hey Tim." I grinned. When I was about to sit on the tattered overstuffed sofa, he stopped me.

"Thatch, I forgot to ask you this on the phone. Are you allergic to dogs? Because Cris now has an emotional support dog that sits in on the sessions."

"Oh, really? I love dogs. Can't wait to meet…"

"Her name is Harmony, and you'll love her. She's been helpful for certain patients, and hopefully Harmony will be a comfort to you as well." Tim said, then placed his hands together like he was praying, and bowed his head. "Cris is ready for you."

"Oh, that was fast," I replied. "Is she still in the same office?"

"Cris's office is at the end of the hallway, the one with the dreamcatcher hanging on the door." He pointed toward her office. "Just walk on in, she's expecting you."

Hanging from her door was a hoop with what appeared to be crude netting inside of it. Bird feathers and brightly colored beads were woven into it. When I opened the door it appeared smoky inside, and an overpowering smell of musk roared up my nostrils.

"Thatch, it's lovely to see you again." Cris beamed at me, and then I saw the source of the smoke. Incense was burning in an elaborate brass thingy, and I recalled how Cris always kept it burning, saying it helped cleanse the spirit.

"You look the same," I commented. Her long brown hair was in a single braid hanging over her left shoulder, and she still had the same granny glasses, similar to the ones John Lennon wore. I held out my hand and she took it in hers, but instead of shaking it, she held it in both hands and shut her eyes.

"I can sense your anxiety," Cris murmured, then opened her eyes and released my hand. "You're in a safe space. Let's begin the healing process." She gestured toward the blue velvet antique couch across from her desk, so I sat. "Let me introduce you to the newest member of Blue Ridge Pride Behavioral Associates, Harmony."

A gorgeous long-haired black chihuahua crawled out from under the couch and stared at me. "Go ahead," Cris directed me. "Pick her up. She loves cuddles."

I leaned over and set her on my lap. Then the little darling got on her hind feet with her paws on my chest and licked my chin. "Aww, what a sweet girl." After the kiss, Harmony curled up on my lap. "What a wonderful way to put your clients at ease."

"Harmony is a rescue. My wife Amber found her at the animal shelter and couldn't resist bringing her home." Amber was one of the therapists working here. "Normally she lives up to her name, but today she got a little feisty with me."

"It's hard to believe this little bundle of fluff could be a bad girl." I cooed while Harmony licked my fingers.

"It's understandable why, so all is forgiven. The vet cancelled her appointment today, so I had to go on YouTube and look up videos on how to express a dog's anal gland." She threw her hands up in the air. "Poor Harmony was past due for it. I managed to get the job done, and saved a ton of money too."

I glanced down at my hands, the ones Cris had just held in

her own. Harmony tilted her tiny head, a questioning look in her eyes. I scanned the room, praying there was a bottle of hand sanitizer somewhere, but there wasn't.

"It was a lot more difficult than I thought. But Harmony is a trooper. So what's going on with you, Thatch?" Cris asked, picking lint from the sleeve of her lavender turtleneck. "The last time we spoke you felt at peace with your ex-husband."

It took a moment for me to get my thoughts together. On the ride here I'd gone over everything I wanted to say, but after learning about Harmony's anal gland it had all flown out of my head.

Cris stared at me with a neutral expression that had always made me feel like I wasn't being judged, while I struggled to get my brain to work. "Dating. Men. Um, there's something wrong with me." I mumbled.

"Go on." Cris murmured, her eyes not leaving mine. "Remember, this is a safe space. Feel free to share whatever you need to."

"I'm fifty-one years old, and I've been divorced for several years. But in all that time I haven't gone on a single date. Finally, a man asked me out, and I'm terrified." I blurted, and Harmony dug into my crotch with her rear leg.

"How does this man make you feel?"

I nudged Harmony to get her to stop kicking my junk, shut my eyes and pictured Joey's face. "He's handsome, with shoulder-length brown hair, and he works as a nurse. But, he's much younger than I am."

"I asked how you felt about him, but you still said something interesting. Do you have issues with this age gap?" Cris asked, and I waved a cloud of smoke out of my face.

"Well, yeah. In my head I know it shouldn't be a problem, but…"

"But, it is." Cris said, a nun's smile settling on her face. "Are you attracted to this man?"

"Kind of?" I mumbled. What did I think about him? It wasn't like I was gaga over Joey. "When I met Brian, my ex-husband, I immediately felt something for him." I laced my fingers through Harmony's hair and began stroking her. "Actually, Brian pissed me off when we first met, but I can't remember what it was."

Cris raised an eyebrow.

"Oh, I remember. It was his attitude. A few weeks later and I couldn't imagine life without him, but Joey is different. He's very nice, good-looking, and, you know, nice." I shrugged my shoulders, wishing I could explain the doubt I felt. Hell, I was a best-selling author, but the correct words escaped me.

"Something is holding you back, right?" Cris asked, then pointed at the coffee table in front of me. "See that piece of obsidian?"

"Um, what is that?"

"It's that shiny piece of black glass. Pick it up and hold it in your hands." I did as instructed, and Harmony growled when I bent over. "Obsidian is a crystal that aids in healing. It possesses energies that help you process emotions. Can you feel the power?"

It felt heavy and smooth, but that was about it. I nodded yes anyway. Who knows? Maybe it was doing something and I was too skeptical to feel it.

"Close your eyes, Thatch."

I did as instructed, and was startled when I heard what sounded like a gong.

"Focus, Thatch." Cris's voice deepened. "How do you actually feel about the man who asked you on a date?"

"Nothing," I blurted. "Like, he's a nice guy, but I feel nothing. He's taking care of the pain in my ass that's living upstairs, so I guess I feel gratitude for his, um, presence."

"You just mentioned that a so-called pain in the ass is living upstairs from you." Cris said, and I opened my eyes. "I'm assuming it means a person."

I nodded.

"Does this person have a name?" Cris asked, and I realized I was still rubbing the stupid glass rock. I set it back on the coffee table, and Harmony growled again.

"Cary Lancaster," I sighed. "He's this guy my son brought home." How the hell could I describe this man and the chaos he'd brought to my life? "To make a long story short, Cary had a medical emergency and he's recuperating in Sam's bedroom. I would send him packing, but his doctor insists on keeping him close by the hospital."

Cris steepled her hands under her chin and shut her eyes for a moment. When she opened them, she asked, "So, this man infuriates you?"

"God yes. Cary is a pompous, stuck-up rich guy who thinks the world revolves around him. He even drives a Rolls Royce. Like, who the hell does that unless you want to flaunt your privilege to the world?" I snapped.

Harmony yipped, then jumped off my lap and scampered under the couch. Cris scribbled something, then pursed her lips. She opened her mouth, shut it again, then spoke.

"Maybe you should reconsider why you are here, Thatch, because it sounds to me like Cary is the source of your angst."

———

AFTERWORD

The Southern Discomfort series was so much fun to write, and Suddenly Single was my favorite. I grew up very near the location of this novel, and many of the little stories I wrote about actually happened. Maybe I'll tell you which ones over a drink one day…

ABOUT THE AUTHOR

Ian O. Lewis is a bestselling author of LGBTQ fiction and romance. He's originally from Richmond, Virginia, but currently calls Mexico home. Follow him on social media and Bookbub to keep up to date with him.